PRAISE FOR MICHAEL G. HICKEY

To L...

I have always felt ~~very~~ fortunate to call you a friend

mike 6/3/2...

Tell Me What You Want

Tell Me What You Want

a novel

Michael G. Hickey

Published by Painted Rock Press, Seattle, Washington
michaelghickeyauthor.com

Edited and designed by Girl Friday Productions
www.girlfridayproductions.com

Cover art: Michael Warlum
Design: Paul Barrett
Project management: Alexander Rigby

ISBN (paperback): 978-0-578-77891-4
ISBN (ebook): 978-0-578-85619-3

For Jon Hutchins

"Forgiveness is the fragrance that the violet sheds on the heel that has crushed it."
—Often attributed to Mark Twain

CONTENTS

ACKNOWLEDGMENTS

I am indebted to numerous individuals, past and present, for their patience and sage advice.

CHAPTER 1

WAITING FOR
LIGHTNING TO STRIKE

In the past, no matter how early Jasper Trueblood dragged himself out of bed, he was always running late. Now, as a college English instructor, nothing could start without him and punctuality was absolutely paramount; otherwise, he began the day with a roomful of restless clock-watchers and methadone-clinic stares. Becoming a teacher meant permanently licking his propensity toward tardiness. It helped to have a job he actually liked. On the way out the door he kissed his fiancée, Daphne, on the forehead. "See you tonight, babe. Don't forget to price some caterers. We need to start planning this wedding."

Daphne, the ever-slumbering but ever-amorous opossum, snatched his hand and pulled him on top of her.

"No!" Jasper yanked his hand free. "I'll be late." He straightened his tie, double-checked his hair in the mirror, and spit on his fingers to tamp down a cowlick tousle gone askew. "I'm giving a test today," he added soberly.

Daphne's beat-up old comforter, a haphazard mélange of carrots and bunny rabbits, was curled up into a tight cocoon. "Fine, Mr. Romance. You're no fun." She pouted, then mumbled into a pillow. "You have no spontaneity."

Jasper resisted the temptation to respond in kind, to initiate an argument that would be left unfinished and waiting to be reheated with last night's tuna casserole. He grabbed his keys.

It was his first car ever: a brand spanking new silver 1989 Honda Accord with racing tires and retractable headlights. Jasper loved to hit the ignition and watch those lizard eyes pop up like matching periscopes every morning, and he recalled how, in retrospect, he had purchased the vehicle rather whimsically because of the James Bond headlights coupled with the fact that he had just been hired to teach English as a Second Language in Seattle. He reasoned he would need reliable transportation inasmuch as he was not a natural-born mechanic like his old man. The payments were steep, but it was an investment in his career. Plus, it had those cool headlights.

Jasper drifted down Queen Anne Hill and submerged into the Battery Street Tunnel. He passed a sputtering pickup truck, cranked up the stereo, and flipped the visor down to escape the menacing glare of the morning sun. Daphne was a bona fide sex maniac. There could be no doubt about that. I'm marrying a sexaholic, he thought. Was it a blessing or a curse? From day one, she had been the insatiable party girl: bottle of booze, five minutes of foreplay, and she'd follow you anywhere. Not that there wasn't a time or place for those things. Just a few years back, Jasper had been a member in good standing of the same club. But now, at age thirty, he had to ask himself if sex, self-medication, and hedonism should monopolize every waking moment. For Daphne, the question was moot. *Party* was a verb, not a noun. It was a way of life. Other than working at The Pillow Factory, her allegiance was right out of the KISS anthem: *I want to rock 'n' roll all night and party every day.*

A sports car cut Jasper off at the exit ramp. Because Seattleites were too polite to honk the horn, Jasper scowled gravely at the driver. For his own part, Jasper no longer had the desire to rock 'n' roll all night nor, for that matter, party every day. "First of all," as he had told Daphne just a few months ago, "I have to get up early. Secondly, after a while, everything loses its fizz, even the world's longest cocktail party. I mean, haven't you read *The Great Gatsby*?" Some of Jasper's old running buddies back in the Midwest still lived lives of endless merriment. What they wanted most out of life was to be struck by lightning, to be successful at business or golf or stud poker or *something*, but they didn't want to stand in the proverbial rainstorm to get it. So, in lieu of taking some demonstrable action to attain it, they continued to rock 'n' roll all night and party every day. Wash, rinse, repeat. This was Daphne, too.

And strangely enough, what were once Daphne's most appealing charms, her endearing little Lolita-esque quirks and eccentricities, even her insatiable lust, had mysteriously evolved into annoying habits of the highest order. Somehow it had all transformed without Jasper really noticing, like the perfect card trick, the imperceptible sleight of hand. And we aren't even married yet, he thought. For example, he once found it altogether amusing and even arousing to watch Daphne parade around the house wearing nothing or next to nothing. At first, he had considered it an altogether likable quality, but in just one year of cohabitation, it had digressed into a subject so volatile as to spark debates about what clothing was suitable at what time of day, the status of the elastic in her undergarments, and whose house it was anyway. Why can't I just let her walk around in her damn underwear? What's the big deal?

Besides lust, he wondered if they even really had anything in common. Daphne had no interest in politics, current events, religion, or sports (unless one could consider shopping a sport, which Jasper did not), and her sole passion for the arts was an obsession with death metal bands featuring names like Bloodcurdling Scream and Dead Babies by Design. Maybe we aren't birds of a feather after all, he thought. Maybe we aren't even flying in the same flock. When he took pause to genuinely reflect, he couldn't recall a recent conversation with her about anything more substantial than what wine to have with dinner or whether to eat outside by the koi pond. Daphne was seven years younger than Jasper, so maybe there was still time. When he'd been twenty-three, Jasper had to admit, the perpetual party mode was still at full throttle. But now, he was avoiding hangovers and concentrating on writing and teaching, which he had come to value more than the revelry. Why am I marrying this woman? he repeated in private moments like a mantra. She was fun and she was funny, but did that constitute matrimony?

Jasper was endlessly grateful to the gods for teaching, to have found something to finance his poetry writing and appease his temperamental muse. It was a noble profession, and though notoriously low paying at a community college, the salary was considerably more than he'd ever made before. In addition, to his surprise, he turned out to be good at it.

His philosophy was akin to the Pygmalion effect—the concept that high expectations lead to high performance. His classroom MO was to pound away relentlessly at the fundamentals until the students, foreigners from a myriad of faraway countries, were muttering them in their sleep, and to tell an occasional joke. Ventriloquism was Jasper's latest hobby. He even went to a downtown magic store and purchased a wooden dummy, which he named Bosworth, after the Seattle Seahawks linebacker Brian Bosworth. The students loved it. They sure never saw anything like this back in Hong Kong or Bangkok.

Suddenly, they think you're a real person. Suddenly, no one wants to miss your class. The dean notices your courses have maximum enrollment plus a waitlist and off-the-chart teacher-course evaluations. In the two years he'd been teaching, Jasper had replaced sexual spontaneity with professional responsibility and discovered it wasn't all that bad. Having not yet relinquished all his vices, he crushed out the joint that he'd been smoking in the ashtray and, at a red light, dotted his eyes with Visine.

Emerald City Community College was a series of cookie-cutter buildings, layered beige brick propped up by concrete pillars, constructed on the cheap back in the seventies. Wrap it in razor wire and it could easily double as a maximum-security correctional facility. At least there were multitudes of flowers in the spring, including sprays of forget-me-nots and deep-blue irises. Jasper spritzed himself with a dash of cologne as he pulled into the parking lot.

* * *

"Good morning, class."

The students, mostly middle-aged refugees, stood in unison. "Good morning, teacher," they said and bowed.

As an adjunct instructor in only his second year, Jasper clung to the lowest vestiges of the teaching totem pole, eagerly accepting the academic scraps left over by the tenured faculty: night classes, Saturday classes, English 101 for vocational students . . . whatever was available. His first course of the day was Introduction to English as a Second Language, Literacy 1-A, composed of adult immigrants in whom the state legislature wanted to develop employable skills and transition to a higher tax bracket.

There were distinct advantages to teaching a course like this: minimal prep time for lesson plans, modest amount of homework to grade, and the students were polite beyond belief. In their countries, teachers were like royalty, figures worthy of honor and respect. Some teachers in their countries were so strict they carried bamboo canes to dole out corporal punishment. The main liability of teaching 1-A was unrelenting exhaustion, like doing three hours of stand-up comedy without a single laugh. They didn't understand humor yet, unless it was physical humor à la Jerry Lewis, thus his ventriloquism. When he took attendance, each student rose resolutely from his or her desk and announced with purpose and pride in various forms of broken English, "Good morning, sir" or "Good morning, Mr. Trueblood."

"Mr. Teacher, sir," said a heavyset, middle-aged Japanese woman with sparse black hair, "my husband cannot be in the school today."

"Why is that, Kiko?" Jasper asked, removing notebooks and flash cards from his briefcase.

"My husband, he is very sick today. He is under the water."

"You mean, *under the weather*?"

She smiled her infectious smile. "Yes, Mr. Teacher, sir."

It was the first week of December, the tail end of fall quarter, and the flowers sprinkled around campus had long since lost their spunk. Although most of the class had made significant progress, a few were still struggling with words like "hello" and "goodbye." A couple might have been cognitively impaired, Jasper wasn't sure. All he knew was that at the end of every Literacy 1-A class, he was ready for a nap. Nevertheless, he kept plugging along and slugging away, and at those precious moments when the light pulsed on and a student's subjects and verbs agreed or they conquered a particular grammar gremlin, he celebrated a tiny victory right along with them.

"Class, what day of the week is it today?"

"Friday," they announced somewhat in sync.

"That's right, Friday. So today, let's talk about future tense. I want to know what you *will do* or what you *are going to do* this weekend. Please answer in future tense, like we practiced yesterday. OK?"

Jasper took Bosworth, his ventriloquism dummy, out of the classroom closet, and stared into his eyes. The students immediately began to laugh. Bosworth wore overalls, a white shirt, and a red bandana tied around a straw hat. "Hi, Bosworth, how are you today?"

"Well, I'm fine, Professor Trueblood. I'm just fine," said Bosworth in his exaggerated drawl.

The class laughed uproariously—the act never got old. The day Jasper bought the dummy from the magic store, he checked out a book from the library called *The Magic of Ventriloquism*. In it, the author made clear that "throwing your voice" was a myth and a physical impossibility. The trick to ventriloquism was practicing speech without moving the lips, and Jasper rehearsed in the mirror every night before bed. To seem believable, one had to practice pronouncing polysyllabic words, especially those starting with *b, f, m, p,* or *v*. But more than anything, one had to perfect the art of body language, of listening and reacting. Facial expressions. One had to convince the audience that the ventriloquist and the puppet were actually having a conversation. Jasper was constantly looking at Bosworth and then doing a double take back at the audience.

"Bosworth, what will you do this weekend?"

"Well, Professor, I will be milkin' my ten cows this weekend."

"Oh, that's great, Bosworth. What else will you do this weekend?"

"I'm going to drink a lot of milk."

The class laughed again and then it was their turn. Some students squinted in synchronized confusion as if speaking a foreign language, which of course they were. Each stood one at a time and, in varying degrees of linguistic dexterity, narrated what life held in store for the next two days. The vast majority mentioned church and cleaning. "Kiko, how about you? What *will* you do this weekend? Please answer in future tense."

Kiko rose from her seat, animated as ever, wearing a pleated maroon skirt and white blouse with a checkerboard pattern on the sleeves. Her coat, which she usually wore during class, was draped over the back of her chair. She smelled like vanilla wafers, and her enunciation was as precise as a Bible Belt preacher on Sunday morning.

"This weekend, teacher, I will go stripping."

Jasper wrinkled his brow. "Say it again, please?"

With great elocution, Kiko spoke louder and more distinctly. "Stripping. This weekend I will be *strip-ping*," she repeated. She smiled, satisfied, and slipped a pencil behind her ear. Kiko was one of the most advanced students in the class, having had several years of English instruction in Japan before World War II, before the entire world combusted around her. Now she was a dutiful wife, mother of four, grandmother of one, and a student again after all these years. Jasper admired Kiko enormously, but of all the activities in which she might be engaged this weekend, he knew stripping was not one.

"Spell the word for me."

Kiko snagged the pencil from behind her ear and wrote in her notebook: s-h-o-p-p-i-n-g.

Careful not to embarrass her, Jasper waited until after class to explain the words' meanings. Kiko blushed and got a healthy chuckle out of it. Of the half-million words in the English language, there were at least two she would never confuse again. Jasper picked up Bosworth. "I sure bet Miss Kiko remembers that word."

Kiko punched Jasper playfully on the shoulder and bowed.

After the three-hour ESL marathon concluded, Jasper had an hour off for lunch. He hit the cafeteria, and as he ate his ham and swiss on sourdough, he searched his briefcase for the stack of English 101 grammar quizzes on fragments and run-ons. To his utter dismay, he discovered that he had neglected to bring them. Shit, he thought. They were still at home on his desk. He had to go get them. Jasper raced home, and when he arrived, he was about to coast into the driveway as usual but, instead, found an unfamiliar vehicle, a white Ford pickup truck with bird crap splattered all over the windshield. He glanced at his wristwatch.

The front door was wide open. As he approached, he heard an assortment of muffled grunts and groans bellowing from the master bedroom. He laid his briefcase on the love seat and tiptoed toward the door. It was opened several inches. Was someone assaulting Daphne? Jasper glanced around the room for a weapon, noticed the golf bag in the corner, and grabbed his lucky seven-iron.

CHAPTER 2

NO LOVE YOU'D CALL REAL

Heart beating in full symphonic percussion, Jasper peeked inside the master bedroom, and on the canopy bed he had paid for in twelve not-so-easy monthly installments, Daphne was writhing in the throes of passion, buck naked in the doggy-style position with her long black spiderweb hair pulled over to the side. She was making that wounded animal sound of hers, and behind her, providing the yin to her yang, was someone Jasper had never seen before—a heavily perspiring man with an inordinate amount of black hair on his back and rear end. Everything seemed decidedly consensual. There was some strange music playing in the background, and Jasper wanted to make note of it as he would be using this entire episode in a future poem. Maybe a book of poems. The song had a distinct drawl and country-and-western twang to it. Since Daphne openly hated and even mocked country and western, this must have been Bigfoot's idea of mood music.

Jasper scanned around as best he could through the slight advantage the door had to offer, looking for any signs of a cowboy hat and, more important, a six-shooter. Seeing none, he took a deep breath and did something every kid raised on bad TV cop shows wanted to do—reared back and kicked the door with all his might. It exploded open with a thunderous *BAM!*

Daphne screamed, throwing herself completely off the bed and into the nearest wall. She reemerged guardedly, wide eyed, head just above the mattress and wrapped in the cyclone of a blue satin sheet. Her furry lover's eyes were alive like two precious gems, his face red, penis erect. He awkwardly turned away, a human sundial, now pointing in the opposite direction. The heavy aroma of sex permeated the atmosphere as diffused light slanted through the window blinds.

Jasper tightened his grip on the golf club and took a swing at a nearby lamp, obliterating it with an eardrum-splitting blow that sent Daphne reeling once again. The head of the golf club got hung up in the lampshade, and Jasper clumsily shook it off. It would have been more theatrical, pyrotechnically speaking, if the lamp had been turned on, but there could be no mistake, he had everyone's attention.

"So, Daph, practicing a little *spontaneity*?" Jasper pivoted around and across the hall, in his office, he saw the stack of English 101 quizzes next to the IBM Selectric typewriter. "Aren't you going to introduce me to your friend?"

"Fuck you."

Jasper smashed the seven-iron into the mirror on the dresser. Shards of glass became diamond-sized projectiles. "I want to know his name!" he screamed.

After an awkward silence, Daphne asked her glistening, cowering paramour, "What was your name again?"

Jasper laughed. "Geez, Daphne, you don't even know the guy's name?" Then it occurred to him—maybe she was a prostitute. Maybe she was turning tricks, and The Pillow Factory was just a ruse. He'd dropped her off there on several occasions last summer when her car had broken down, but . . . Was he about to marry a real-life hooker?

Finally, in an apparent gesture of goodwill, Daphne's lover sheepishly reached out and extended his sizable paw. "My name is William."

Jasper shook it impulsively and felt better for having done so, though immediately wiped his hand on his pants to avoid any residual love goo.

"Hi, Bill. May I call you Bill?" Jasper asked. "Some people don't like nicknames, you know. They prefer to be addressed by their given names."

"I prefer William."

"Oh, for Chrissakes," Daphne moaned.

"Fair enough, William. I'm Jasper. By the way, her name is Daphne." He motioned toward his soon-to-be ex-fiancée. "I'm not exactly sure how far you two have gotten in terms of formal introductions." He shot her a cold stare, an evil glare that drained the blood from his face. He saved it for occasions just like this, though in reality, it was mostly just an act. Now that he thought about it, his chemistry and Daphne's had proved to be incompatible a long time ago. At least she had the guts to make the first move.

"Sorry, man," William said. "She never told me nothin' about no husband."

"Oh, we aren't married, William, nor will we ever be. Feel free to get her phone number, if you'd like, so you two can resume your little rendezvous."

"I fucking hate you, Jasper Trueblood."

"Ah," Jasper said. "Jezebel lashes out. I'll get to you in a minute, sweet pea." He returned his attention to William. "See,

William, right now, Daphne and I are about to have a spat. An old-fashioned lovers' quarrel. Then we're going to officially cancel our wedding plans and terminate our relationship. Frankly, we've been putting it off for quite a while. Oh, there'll be the usual haranguing and finger-pointing . . . that sort of thing. You know the drill, right, William? I mean, everyone's walked through this fire at one point or another. But hey, after we finish with the exit strategy, you can dress up like Little Bo Peep and pretend like she's one of your sheep for all I care."

Without further incident, William expeditiously managed to step into his trousers, snatch up the rest of his apparel, and rapidly retreat out the front door, with the squeal of tires on asphalt sealing the deal.

There was a pause. Then, "Nice guy, that William," Jasper said.

"I seriously hate you," said Daphne.

"Did you happen to notice that he had an extremely large dick?"

"You're such a conceited asshole."

Jasper checked his watch. He didn't have time to fight, which seemed to further infuriate her. Finally, she rolled over on her hip and faced the opposite wall, whimpering softly.

He dropped the seven-iron and sat next to her on the bed. "Daphne, maybe it's just me, but I don't think things are working out between us." And just because he was curious, he was going to ask if she really was a nymphomaniac, but now that he'd made his point, he just wanted it to be over.

Daphne turned and gave him the best puppy dog look she could muster.

Jasper checked his watch again. He would be late for class if he didn't leave in four minutes or less. "Aren't you worried about getting pregnant? Or AIDS or STDs? I mean, that guy wasn't even wearing a rubber. Do you really want to give birth to William's hairy little love chinchilla?"

"I'm allergic to latex, and lambskin is disgusting. You're disgusting," Daphne groaned. "And I'm allergic to you. You used to pay attention to me. You used to cuddle me and say sweet things." She sniffled. "Why did you stop cuddling me? Why don't you love me anymore?"

Ironically, Jasper always thought he'd be a cuddler, ever since being deflowered all those years ago in college by his first real sweetheart, Lani Sablan from the island of Guam. For years, he used to repeat that line over and over, day and night, recite it in his dreams, write it on the cover of his notebook in dazzling cursive, sing it in the shower—*Lani Sablan from the island of Guam.* The only girl he had ever really loved. Just saying her name gave him a shot of adrenaline like a firefighter carrying a baby from a burning building. *Lani Sablan.* He'd give anything to see old Lani again: her silky jet-black hair, hypnotic blue eyes, million-dollar smile. And her hands, her incredibly sculpted hands, soft and supple as a heart surgeon's. He'd cuddled like crazy with Lani, that is, until she moved back home to tend to her ailing daddy. For the millionth time he wondered, whatever happened to Lani Sablan from the island of Guam? He'd forgotten how much he missed her. To be honest, there hadn't been much cuddling at all since Lani. He had to give her a call sometime. "I'm curious, Daph, and I'm not asking this to be an asshole, but do you consider yourself a nymphomaniac?"

"You idiot, I'm bored out of my mind. I'm so sick of you and your stupid job. You come home and tell me all your precious little teaching stories, like anyone gives a shit. They're boring as hell. *You're* boring as hell."

"Are you a nymphomaniac?"

"Shut up."

"You once told me you were kicked out of a sleepover in third grade because you got caught telling the other girls what a blow job was."

"You know what your problem is?" Daphne said. "You think you're better than everybody else. And guess what. You're not. You ain't even close. And you're a hack poet, too."

Jasper laughed. "*A hack poet.* Ha! That's funny, Daphne. When we met, you said a poem had to rhyme to be a poem. That's how much you knew about poetry. Now, suddenly, you're a literary critic?" He inhaled, exhaled, then lowered his tone. "OK, seriously, all kidding aside, tell me how you met William. Does he work at The Pillow Factory?"

"None of your business. And I don't want to marry you anyway. You're fat, and you keep getting fatter every day."

Ouch, Jasper thought, looking at his paunch in the mirror. He took the liberty of removing the keys from her key chain that she would no longer need. "Now we're getting personal, huh? Look, you can have the bed. I'll burn it if you don't take it, so you might as well get someone to haul it over to your sister's place."

"I am *not* going back to live with Monica!" Daphne said. She began dressing in a newfound burst of angry energy, savagely pulling on garments the way women did when they were pissed off. "That bitch insults my intelligence. Just 'cause I don't have a college degree don't mean I'm not smart. She's just like you! You both think I'm some dumb hick jus' 'cause I didn't go to college. What makes poetry better than death metal anyway? Just 'cause you say it is? Fuck you. Fuck all y'all!"

"Out of curiosity, Daphne, how many other Williams have there been?"

"Gaaawd," she said in exasperation like air being let out of a balloon. "This was the only time. And the only reason I couldn't remember his name was because I get it mixed up with Philip, another guy who works on the loading dock. There, I said it, yes, William works at The Pillow Factory. William and Philip, the names sound alike. Are you happy now? Are you satisfied? You're such an asshole."

"Baby, look, I don't care if you stay with Monica or William or take the ferry over to Bremerton and fuck the entire Seventh Fleet." He walked up to her, held her alabaster face in his hands, and for a moment considered twisting her head off like a bottle cap. "We had some laughs, but it's over now." He kissed her on the forehead. "You deserve better than me anyway."

She sniffled some more. "Can I really have the bed?"

"Yes. The sheets, too. I insist. No hard feelings."

"I could tell William was pretty scared when you smashed that lamp. His knees were shakin' really bad."

Jasper smiled a little. "I always hated that lamp."

He sped back to school, arrived with three minutes to spare, and proctored his English test. That evening, Daphne's brother-in-law came over with a truck and hauled away the bed as well as the rest of her meager belongings, mostly clothes, shoes, and the love seat. They left Jasper's small house on the top of Queen Anne Hill with bed in tow, everything loosely tied together with yellow bungee cord like a poorly wrapped Christmas present.

Later that night, Jasper sat alone in the living room for hours with the lights off and the radio on, steeped deep in despair, self-pity, and melancholy cocktails. He missed his mother—both of them, in fact—his biological mother, Connie, and his adoptive mother, Doris. He realized he had no real friends in Seattle. It was like the Van Halen song: *I got no love, no love you'd call real. Ain't got nobody waitin' at home.*

He started to call his father back in the Midwest. He hung up, called again, hung up again. He hadn't spoken to dear old Dad in months, hadn't even wished him a happy birthday last May, just left a message on the answering machine. He thought he had forgiven the old man a decade ago for all the violence and vitriol, but can one ever truly forgive what one can never truly forget? His father's mercurial temper, leather belt, and *spare the rod, spoil the child* policy continued to plague Jasper's psyche, even though his father had atoned and apologized years ago. Still . . . it was hard to let go, hard not to hate, hard to dismiss breaking a vase at age ten and the customary lowering of the trousers and underwear, bending over the coffee table, being whipped with three lashes of the leather belt, and three more if he cried even a little. Jasper grew up in a crime-and-punishment household during a crime-and-punishment era. Even now, decades later, there was that unmistakably male voice in the background of his brain saying, *"Stop crying, you little pussy. Big boys don't cry."*

As for his adoptive mother, Doris, she didn't believe in corporal punishment but did have her own views on the administration of discipline. When Jasper was a child and threw a tantrum because he didn't get his way, like wanting a candy bar or a new toy, Doris forced him to sit in "the feelings chair," a wicker rocker in the spare bedroom. There were no books, no toys, and no TV allowed. Doris believed it was important for children to feel their feelings, and she wanted Jasper to feel his, but he also had to understand that the rest of the world didn't necessarily have to share his discomfort. In the feelings chair, Jasper could rant, rave, cry, and scream if he wanted, and when he was finished, he was encouraged to join the family for dinner or to play a board game. Now, as Jasper sat in his living room and stared out the picture window into the darkness, he leaned back in his black leather BarcaLounger, his new feelings chair. Then he did something he hadn't done in years, cried a gut-wrenching sob.

* * *

Eight days after the breakup, late on a Friday afternoon, the old sting of bachelorhood had set in. He was in his office at school, staring blankly out the window at the parking lot. If he could finish grading this stack of English 101 essays, he'd have his weekend free to write poems, do laundry, and purchase a new bed—the futon having wrecked what had formerly been his spinal column. He was recording scores in his grade book when Margaret, the matronly receptionist and administrative assistant to the dean, passed by.

"Good night, Professor Trueblood. Have a wonderful weekend."

"You too, Margaret. Do you have any plans?" They spoke briefly about Christmas shopping and the upcoming holidays. In his short stint at the college, Jasper learned to treat secretaries with the utmost respect and to send little gifts during Secretary Week. For answers on the administrative code, policy, procedure, or how to navigate the halls of academe, they were the puppeteers working the marionettes behind the curtain. The real ventriloquists. And just as Margaret was about to step out the door, a thought hit Jasper like an inside fastball. "Margaret, may I ask you a favor?"

"Certainly," she said with her trademark charm and alacrity, buttoning up her coat and wrapping her muffler around her neck.

"I have to make a long-distance phone call, and it's kind of urgent. If I absolutely promise to limit the call to five minutes and give you my word that I'll never use it again, do you think I could have the long-distance access code?"

Margaret squinted into his eyes. "Is there a problem, Professor?"

Jasper nodded. "Yes. Please, Margaret. Five minutes, max."

She hesitated. "Well, all right, but just this once. Make the call from my phone. Dean Wright frowns on the unauthorized use of the access code."

"Thank you. Thank you very much."

Margaret smiled. "OK, I hope everything's all right."

She dialed the number, and as she closed the door, Jasper punched 411 and waited for an operator. "Yes, operator, this is for the island of Guam. I'd like the number for a Miss Lani Sablan." During the crackling overseas silence, Jasper wondered what the chances were that she would even be on Guam after all these years. A hundred to one? A thousand to one?

"OK, sir, I found an L. Sablan in Agana, Guam. Would you like that number?"

"Yes." Jasper swallowed hard. All his neurotransmitters and nerve endings sparked up like a welding torch. He suddenly remembered the name of her city was pronounced "ah-gahn-nya," not the flat "ah-gah-nah" he'd just heard from the operator.

The operator gave him the number and repeated it once again. "For an additional seventy-five cents, would you like me to connect you?"

"Yes, please. That would be much appreciated." He remembered it was technically the next day in Guam. He also recalled something his father used to say about being "a day late and a dollar short."

And as the ringing of the connection began, he heard the operator say, "Thank you, sir."

There was a click on the line. "Hello?"

"Uh, hello." It didn't sound like Lani. "Is Lani Sablan there, please?"

"No, she's at work. This is Susan, her sister. Who's this?"

"Oh, uh, hi. This is Jasper Trueblood. I'm an old friend of Lani's from college, back from the University of Arizona days."

"Hi. She'll be back in a couple hours. You want me to have her call you?"

"No, that's OK. I kinda want to surprise her. I'll just try back in a couple hours if that's all right."

"OK, sure. Suit yourself. Bye-bye."

But instead of calling back, Jasper came up with a masterful, category-five brainstorm. He would travel to Guam over Christmas break and "accidentally" bump into Lani at a mall or a restaurant or a grocery store. Of course, after nearly a decade, it was safe to assume that romantically, she was married or otherwise attached. Nevertheless, he didn't care. He wasn't trying to steal her; he just wanted to see her. At least he knew she still lived on Guam, and at the end of the day, he was just an old college friend who happened to be on the island by chance for a teaching conference or to visit some long-lost cousin and then *oh my God, I can't believe it . . . is it really you? What a surprise to see you!* It'd do his soul a world of good just to look at those baby blues one more time and hold those surgeon-like hands. *Lani Sablan from the island of Guam.*

Jasper went home and searched through boxes in the closet until he found his passport. He called the first travel agent he found in the phone book and checked on the price of a round-trip ticket to Guam, which, it turned out, would deplete a sizable chunk of the money he had unexpectedly inherited when Connie died and left him the house and IRA. That night, he smoked the rest of his weed and drank a bottle of Cold Duck. He was on a mission. He could feel the earth revolve on its axis. Every breath was like being born anew because it was completely out of character to do something so wild, so impulsive, so . . . expensive. He hadn't done anything like this since he bought the lizard-eyed Honda. When he finally got to sleep, he dreamed about cuddling with Lani Sablan from the island of Guam. It was tropical and exotic and erotic and the best dream ever. When he woke up the next day, he even called his father.

Fortunately, there was no answer.

CHAPTER 3

RAY'S PLEASURE PALACE

Three days before Jasper was scheduled to depart for his most ambitious (or foolhardy) adventure ever, a Pacific island scavenger hunt in search of the elusive Miss Lani, he had already turned in his fall quarter grades and next quarter's syllabi to Margaret. Rumor had it that within twelve months, all instructors at Emerald City Community College would have their own computer, and grades would be submitted electronically. Most forms of communication would be electronic as well, replacing paper memos. Jasper took great pride in his prognostication that the pending Computer Age was destined to be an abject failure and predicted that personal computers, cellular telephones, and most technology in general would soon be a subject of nostalgia, like pogo sticks and pet rocks. Also, he had to remember not to drink so much while grading papers. His comments became increasingly illegible, unintelligible, and more or less hieroglyphic.

The final 101 assignment was always a research paper on a controversial subject, an exercise in analytical and critical thinking. Fortunately, this term he had not detected any instances of plagiarism, unlike last quarter when one student had clearly lifted several lines from other sources, a poorly constructed academic pastiche without proper attribution or citation. When Jasper called him on it, the student replied with great sincerity, "Professor Trueblood, I swear I did not plagiarize that essay. But I think my roommate did."

As a lover of language, Jasper kept a notebook of his favorite student-generated malapropisms as well as dangling participles and misplaced modifiers. His 101 class had fewer of these linguistic faux pas than his Literacy 1-A group, but still there was the occasional misstep in diction and syntax. His favorite from last quarter was from a righteous, self-avowed born-again Christian named Glenn. *Pre-marital sex results in big black sores on your gentiles.* To which Jasper had responded glibly, "I think you mean *genitals* as I doubt that our Jewish brothers and sisters would be immune from this scourge." Then a student named Becky weighed in on capital punishment. *The death penalty is an excellent detergent to crime.* And later in the same essay: *multiple studies have shown that executed murderers are far less likely to become repeat offenders than are living murderers.* But Jasper's favorite line from the entire year was quite intentional, from a student writing on the topic of school uniforms. *It seems the only thing two experts can agree on is how wrong the third expert is.*

It had been two and a half weeks since Jasper kicked Daphne out of the house for her extracurricular activities, and since then, he had been lonely as hell. He was already desperate enough to call and propose a grudge fuck. His days consisted mostly of smoking dope, drinking rum, and masturbating. And she was right—he did look fat. Once a day he stood in front of the full-length mirror in the bathroom and sucked in his gut to no avail. His hairline was receding, and crow's feet spread from the corners of his eyes. If this was thirty, he cringed at forty and beyond. For certain, Lani would not be seeing the tanned college kid he had been in Arizona. He wondered if she looked the same.

Jasper decided to clean out his collection of pornography. Anything with stuck pages was automatically deep-sixed. Altogether, he trashed twelve *Playboys*, seven *Penthouses* (including one *Penthouse Forum*), four *Hustlers*, three *Ouis*, two *Gallerys*, one *High Society*, and a *Playgirl* (Daphne's). Jasper noted that the guys in *Playgirl* never seemed fully cognizant that they were naked, as if exposing their peashooters was something they did on a regular basis. The handsome cowboy on the cover wore nothing but a black Stetson, black leather chaps, and a toothy grin. The caption read, "Mr. September— clearly not his first rodeo!" Jasper was not finished with smut, not by any means. He just needed a new collection. There were also two errands to run before his 5,663-mile excursion to the island of Guam, and the first was to his dope dealer.

Christopher was in his early forties, gay, blond, muscle-bound as a Greek statue, and lived with his boyfriend, John, who was a waiter at the Four Seasons. Christopher was a dead ringer for that handsome cowboy on the cover of *Playgirl*, sans the Stetson. His ganja was the best Jasper had ever smoked. It was also the most expensive. Good weed in Seattle was $40 for an eighth of an ounce. Christopher's was $50 for an eighth, $95 for a quarter, $185 for a half, and $350 for an entire ounce. It was called "skunk weed" because it smelled just like a dead skunk. Jasper could smoke half a number in the morning and be buzzed all day.

Christopher lived on Alki Beach, one of Seattle's most breathtaking landscapes, where the Space Needle, ferries, and downtown skyline were visible just across Elliott Bay. Joggers, rollerbladers, and skateboarders traversed the sidewalks day and night. During spring and summer, the aromatic smell of barbecue wafted among the pine trees. Beachcombers were ubiquitous, volleyball games commonplace, and picture-postcard sunsets were a regular guest on the horizon. Christopher resided in a spacious condominium with bay windows overlooking the beach, and he drove a brand-new BMW. In Seattle, the marijuana trade was extremely lucrative. His exclusive brand of smoke was allegedly grown in a basement by two Mother Earth lesbians who chanted to their plants before dawn every morning.

The routine was always the same. First, the buyer would call Christopher and place the order for one, two, three, or four "tickets," which in dope code translated to an eighth, quarter, half, or full ounce of product. There was never to be any mention of drugs on the phone, and Christopher was adamant that the buyer had a thirty-minute window to arrive—no more, no less. Christopher did not want multiple clients at his house concurrently, as if the neighbors were somehow unaware of the constant foot traffic. Then he would greet the customer at the door, go to his safe under the kitchen sink, click in the combination, and extract a gallon-sized Ziploc bag filled with the green menace. He would subsequently weigh it on a high-tech digital scale in plain view, that way the buyer could clearly see there was no skimming. Quality and reliability were Christopher's trademarks. Then he would count out the money bill by bill while his client stood watching. He did not give change or credit, so it was essential to bring exact cash. Jasper was always in and out in less than ten minutes. He had known Christopher for over a year, yet it was still awkward to fabricate casual conversation.

"It looks like it might rain," Jasper would say.

"Uh-huh," Christopher would reply without making eye contact.

"Got any plans today?"

"Just going to the gym. You?"

"Maybe do some laundry."

And so on.

Jasper always brought a Tupperware container, so Christopher didn't have to waste his baggies. Then Jasper would go home, turn on the living room lamp, spread the dope out on a cafeteria tray, and cut it up with scissors into something rollable. Jasper didn't like bongs or pipes—they killed his lungs. He would use his orange Zig-Zag rolling papers to twist the weed into joints that resembled unfiltered cigarettes, then he'd lick them and let them dry, so they'd burn evenly. Over the years, he'd become a bona fide *twist-ologist*.

After Jasper smoked a little more than usual, he set out for his other pre-Guam errand, a sleazy little peep show down south near the airport that he'd been meaning to investigate since even before he broke up with Daphne. There were plenty of adult arcades closer to home, but he was afraid he would run into someone from school. One thing about this city, no matter what you were into, Seattle had plenty of it, and on the down-low if desired.

The place was called Ray's Pleasure Palace, a seedy, pornographic diorama of carnal intrigue, infamous for its risqué marquee. In line with the season, today's sign read: MERRY XXX-MAS!

The parking lot was three-quarters full, and it was only the middle of the afternoon. Jasper wore a baseball cap to hide his eyes. Near the marquee was a blinking sign—LIVE GIRLS GIRLS GIRLS—as well as white neon lights outlining the curvaceous pink silhouette of a twelve-foot woman sporting voluptuous breasts, long legs, and a left eye with an enormous palm-frond eyelash that winked seductively on and off. Jasper was still a good Catholic boy at heart, and his heart was tapping double-time to remind him of that. He thought of a title for a new poem, "Libido Incognito." He had to remember to write that down. Stealthily opening the thick wooden front door and closing it gently behind him, Jasper slipped from the daylight into a blinding, bluish-black darkness.

Ray's was, to be sure, a full-service pleasure palace. At the end of a barely lit dark corridor featuring posters of voluptuous women in the lewdest of poses, there was a cigarette machine, a token changer, and a long glass display case. The place was packed. At least twenty men, mostly older than Jasper, loitered around the magazine racks and ogled the collection of VHS tapes, featuring *Judy the Virgin Nymph* and *The Adventures of Captain Lust*. There were dildos of every size and color, vibrators, french ticklers, lingerie, negligees, a condom bin, and a life-size blow-up doll with an open mouth that formed a capital *O*.

Outside the main floor were two doors: Live Peeps and Video Peeps.

"How much is it?" Jasper asked in a deep tone, a feeble attempt to disguise his voice.

The clerk, long and lean with a blond mullet, wore black leather pants and a white Ray's Pleasure Palace T-shirt. He was methodically stroking his walrus mustache while watching a soap opera on a portable TV that was on the counter next to him.

"The video booths are three and a half minutes for a dollar. The private booths are a dollar a minute. You have to use tokens. The token machine is over there. It takes tens, fives, and ones."

Jasper got ten bucks' worth and headed back toward Live Peeps. On the wall was a sign that read One Person per Booth, and adjacent to the curtain was a photo montage of all the girls, a smorgasbord of salaciousness for every taste: thin, thick, tall, short, blonde, brunette, redhead. He remembered Miss Kiko had confused the word *stripping* for *shopping*. In Booth 12, the last one, was a black girl with strawberry-blonde dreads named "Ginger Snap," the only one smiling. Cute dimples, too.

Jasper pushed open the curtain and walked inside the back room. It was even darker than the showroom, and creepy old perverts were slithering all over the place, trying not to make eye contact. It occurred to Jasper that he was now an official member of this club himself: the "c.o.p. club" (a.k.a. creepy old perverts). A voice in the back of his head told him he was deteriorating faster than he could lower his standards.

Outside each booth, a red light was either on or off, similar to parochial school when every Friday the kids walked from the classrooms over to the church for confession. It was understood that if a red light was on, the confessional was occupied by a priest and repentant sinner. Ray's Pleasure Palace was confession in reverse.

He walked toward Booth 12. The light was off. He stepped inside the door. It clicked shut behind him. Jasper could barely see the coin slot; everything was so cave-like. He slid in several tokens, which activated a black plastic shutter that ascended with a pneumatic swoosh. And there she was, sitting behind a Plexiglas window: the illustrious Miss Ginger Snap. She picked up the red phone. "Hi, honey," she said. The raspy contours of her dreamy voice were one part Marilyn Monroe and one part hostage negotiator. "I'm Ginger Snap."

Jasper picked up the red phone on his side of the glass. "Hi," he said. "I'm Jasper." And he immediately regretted giving his real name.

"Sit down and make yourself comfortable."

"Yeah," Jasper said, wiping perspiration from his brow. Could she tell how nervous he was? "OK."

Ginger Snap smiled that killer smile from the photo. Her eyes were yellowish amber, tawny like a cat. She appeared to be in her twenties and had the same blonde dreadlocks from the photo. She also had the cutest dimples and whitest teeth he had ever seen. She wore raspberry-red lipstick, a gold cross necklace, and gold hoop earrings. Once Jasper's eyes adjusted to the backlight, he could see her smooth cocoa skin and her outfit—a sexy red lace bustier that was barely able to harness her breasts. She also wore a red garter belt, red satin G-string, and red thigh-high fishnet stockings with black stiletto heels to complete the ensemble.

"Wow," Jasper said. "You're even prettier than your picture."

She smiled again. "Well, aren't you sweet? Why don't you take off your jacket and stay awhile?"

Jasper took a deep breath, removed his windbreaker, and sat on the leather-cushioned bench behind him. A timer noted that he had sixty seconds left, so he slipped the rest of the tokens in the slot.

"Tell me what you want."

"Whatever you got," Jasper said. He hung up the phone.

Ginger hung up in tandem on her side of the glass and turned music on at a low volume, "She Drives Me Crazy" by the Fine Young Cannibals. She started to shift her hips and turned so she was facing the mirrored glass behind her. She unfastened her bustier in back and slowly, tantalizingly, exposed her large brown breasts and dark nipples. Smiling again, she seductively removed the top altogether and tossed it behind her.

Jasper could feel himself starting to get sparked.

"Daddy likes?"

Jasper nodded. "Yes, ma'am. Very much." He wasted no time in unzipping his jeans. She had a way of rolling her hips and jiggling her peach-shaped derriere that was altogether intoxicating. Two songs later, Jasper knew he was very close to climax when the timer showed he had sixty seconds left. He reached for his wallet when he remembered that he'd spent everything else at Christopher's. "Aw, shit!" he said, jacking off harder and faster. But before he came, the timer inched toward zero, and the partition started to lower. Ginger Snap ducked down, winked, blew a kiss, waved goodbye.

After the coitus interruptus, Jasper couldn't wait to get back home and finish the job. As he left Ray's Pleasure Palace, he strangely did not feel guilt, shame, or any of that old-time religion. He wondered if anyone ever fell in love with the girls in the peeps. There was something liberating about not having to talk afterward, about not having to discuss the bills or the boss or the weather. He just had to remember to bring more money.

* * *

The next day Jasper went right back to Ray's, this time bringing twenty-seven dollars. The marquee read: KISS ME UNDER THE CAMELTOE.

Jasper got his tokens and when he walked behind the curtain, there were a few c.o.p.'s loitering around, though not as many as the day before. He noticed the light on over Booth 12. It was almost twenty minutes before some old scuzzball with wavy salt-and-pepper hair walked out wearing a Green Bay Packers jacket. The zipper to his trousers was still down.

Jasper fed the machine all his tokens.

"Tell me what you want," Ginger said.

"Hi, it's me. I was here yesterday, but I ran out of tokens."

"I remember." She smiled. "Jasper."

Oh, what the hell, Jasper thought, so she knows my real first name. "I stocked up on tokens today." He sat down. There was music again, this time "Long Cool Woman in a Black Dress" by the Hollies, and appropriately enough Ginger Snap was wearing a black silk teddy and black fishnet gloves to go along with the gold cross necklace. He'd smoked a lot of weed and felt more emboldened than the day before. "I'll tell you exactly what I want, Miss Ginger Snap. I want to watch you touch yourself."

Ginger smiled again. Jasper loved her dimples.

She started to dance and shimmy her lush body, all the way from those strawberry-blonde dreads down to her peachy hips. She unfastened her teddy and discarded it. As it dropped to the floor, Jasper felt that old valentine inside his shirt kick into gear. She fondled her breasts, pushed them together, and then licked one of them. She squinted at him through the glass and mouthed, "They're real." Then she started to reach between her legs as she writhed to the music. She picked up the phone. "Is this what you want, Daddy?"

Jasper nodded. He licked his hand, and in no time, he could feel it coming. His left leg began to shake. There was a box of tissues on the counter, but Jasper didn't get to them in time. When it was over, heart pounding, he sat down to catch his breath. It was the most amazing climax he'd had in ages, maybe ever. He had this inexplicable urge to tell her he loved her. "Thank you," he mouthed into the glass at the one-minute warning.

She bent down and smiled, winked, blew him a kiss, waved goodbye—apparently her signature send-off.

As he drove home, Jasper couldn't stop fantasizing about Ginger Snap and her catchphrase, "Tell me what you want." Sometimes he would say it to himself and think about her. *Ginger Snap.* Behind the glass, who was she really? Where was she from? Who did she love? What color was her sky? What did *she* want? Jasper needed an X-ray to look at her from the inside out. He was wet cement; she was a pair of bare feet walking.

CHAPTER 4

ILLUSIONS AT THIRTY THOUSAND FEET

It was December 21, 1989, and Jasper was scheduled to leave for Guam in less than three hours. It began to dawn on him what a ludicrous gamble this was, not only the exorbitant cost but also the notion that Lani would even remember him. She was probably married, gay, or suffering from amnesia. Perhaps she had left Guam for the holidays. Perhaps she had simply written off the Tucson years altogether. He didn't even know her address. In any case, the plane ticket to paradise was paid for, and if nothing else, it would be a much-needed dream vacation on a tropical island in the Pacific. What's the worst that could happen? he thought.

He knocked on the neighbor's door. Mrs. McCready was a retired ER nurse and longtime widow who often babysat her grandkids. She came to the door wearing a canary-yellow muumuu.

"Professor Trueblood, come right on in." Mrs. McCready's living room was jam-packed from floor to ceiling with every conceivable bauble, bead, bric-a-brac, knickknack, curio, conversation piece, objet d'art, souvenir, and houseplant imaginable, which were all vulnerable and at significant risk when her grandkids came to visit.

"Are you excited for your big trip?"

"I am," Jasper said. "A little nervous, too."

"Would you like some peppermint tea?"

"No, thank you. The shuttle van'll be here any minute. I just wanted to drop off the key. I'd like you to keep it even after I come back. And here's the fish food for the koi pond. They don't eat much during the winter, so maybe just a healthy pinch every four or five days. If you can't see them, don't worry. They like to hide at the bottom where it's warmer."

"The grandkids all love your koi pond." Mrs. McCready shushed her parakeet, chirping away in a cage next to the picture window. "Now when will you be back?"

"I'm not entirely sure. It's an open-ended ticket, but school starts on Tuesday the second, so I'll probably be back by New Year's Eve at the latest. I actually gain a day on the way back when I cross the international date line." Jasper recalled he had once published a poem titled "Counterclockwise."

"Tell me again, why Guam?"

"I dated a girl in college named Lani. I'm going there to surprise her. I'm not expecting a romance novel or anything, I'd just like to see her again. That was nine years ago. I'm not sure she'll even remember me."

Mrs. McCready gave Jasper a hug and wished him good luck. "She'll remember. Women never forget those kinds of things. And don't worry, I've got everything under control around here. Would you like a little snack for the plane? I tried a new recipe for my fruitcake, topped it with marzipan. It's absolutely to die for."

"That would be lovely." He really didn't, but he also didn't want to insult her.

Jasper went home, locked the doors, and double-checked the defective window in the living room near the koi pond that was floor-level and where someone had once tried to break in. A few minutes later, the shuttle van drove Jasper out to the airport with three other strangers. They eventually cruised right past Ray's Pleasure Palace, sporting the marquee du jour: OUT WITH THE OLD, IN WITH THE NUDE.

"Flight 917 is now ready for boarding at Gate Three."

Jasper was getting more anxious with each passing hour. His derring-do and esprit de corps were beginning to wane. It was a nine-hour flight to Tokyo, a four-hour layover, and then another four hours to Guam. Normally, if it were just a domestic flight, he would have smuggled a little pill bottle filled with perfectly rolled joints in his underwear, but he didn't want to test his luck going through customs.

He settled in on the plane, stared out the window, and slept intermittently. He watched a couple of in-flight movies, then read the newspaper. The headline read "US Invades Panama." Apparently, the American government and President George Herbert Walker Bush, a former CIA and FBI director, didn't appreciate the way Manuel Noriega was playing both ends against the middle in the volatile cocaine wars. Halfway through reading the article, Jasper heard the primal screams of an infant behind him. She was maybe a year old and delivered a couple of swift karate kicks to the back of Jasper's seat. As the super-lunged baby cried wildly, akin in volume to an air-raid siren, passengers started to look at one another and roll their eyes. Jasper could hear the child's mother trying to pacify the kid with a juice box.

"Megan, your diaper is dry. What's wrong, honey? Tell Mommy what's wrong."

A stewardess dropped by to see if she could assist, but the mother was at a loss. Clearly what the little one wanted more than anything was to get off this damn airplane and onto solid ground. After a while, Jasper remembered he'd brought Bosworth in his carry-on. He knew he must have brought his sidekick for something, and her name was Megan.

"Ma'am," he said, now standing in the aisle, "if you don't mind, I have something little Megan might enjoy." He reached into the overhead compartment, extracted his carry-on, and pulled out his ventriloquism dummy. Ironically, he almost hadn't brought it but changed his mind at the last minute. "Look, Bosworth, the baby wants to go home. The baby doesn't want to eat any more stinking pretzels."

Bosworth responded in kind with his Texas twang, "Hey, Professor, should I tell the baby a joke?"

"OK, Bosworth, but you gotta keep it clean."

Bosworth paused. "Aw, Professor, but I don't know any clean jokes."

"Boooooosworth . . ."

"OK, OK, I know one clean joke."

"Good."

"Two lesbians walk into a bar—"

"Bosworth!"

The child stopped crying and stared wide eyed at the dummy, then at Jasper, then back at the dummy. The mother smiled, too, and several passengers on the periphery took notice. They laughed and pointed, and pretty soon, the entire plane was in on it.

Bosworth continued, "In the event of a water landing, Miss Megan, don't worry. Sharks eat the big people first. More meat."

The flight attendants gathered around.

"And always remember to secure your oxygen mask before assisting your mommy. Hey, Megan, wanna barf in the airsick bags?"

The baby grinned and bounced up and down and began waving her arms.

"Oh, look, Professor, Megan's trying to fly. Did you see her flap her wings? Maybe she's part eagle. By the way, Professor, ya think one of those lovely flight attendants might want to get Uncle Bosworth a refreshing adult beverage? Like maybe a double Bacardi and Diet Coke? And perhaps a chocolate chip cookie for Miss Megan?"

There was more laughter from the crowd, and even some passengers from first class clambered back to coach to investigate the commotion. Jasper switched seats with a man directly across the aisle from Megan and her mom, enjoyed a few complimentary cocktails, and engaged the baby in conversation off and on until she fell asleep.

On the descent toward Tokyo, the captain announced on the public address system, "Ladies and gentlemen, let's give a nice round of applause for our entertainers extraordinaire, the professor and Uncle Bosworth!"

There was an enthusiastic ovation. Jasper looked dramatically at Bosworth, Bosworth responded in kind, and they bowed in unison with great flourish. The clapping went on for several minutes, and when the plane finally touched down, the mom gave Jasper a big hug and kiss on the cheek.

"Hey," Bosworth said, "I want some of that!"

There was muffled laughter.

When the plane de-boarded, two official-looking airline personnel in blue uniforms approached Jasper and offered him a first-class upgrade for the connecting flight to Guam. Jasper graciously accepted. More free cocktails.

* * *

After the four-hour layover and boarding his final connecting flight, Jasper waited for takeoff and reviewed the pertinent facts he had researched about Guam in the *Encyclopaedia Britannica*. His favorite was that the natives built these totally radical canoes. There were also bodacious white-sand beaches and "swaying palm trees surrounded by cerulean water."

By the time he finally touched down, exhausted from all the pressurization, depressurization, in-flight performing, and general apprehension, Jasper was too debilitated to do anything but go to the hotel and crash. Guam International Airport had only one terminal, and getting through customs was a breeze compared to Tokyo. Once Jasper retrieved his bags, he waited in the designated area for the next taxi. The Guamanian and American flags stood like sentries, flapping and fluttering atop fifty-foot metal poles in the front entrance. He was the most bone-weary he'd ever been in his life, even more so than when he hadn't slept for five days after his mother died in '78. Without Christopher's high-grade marijuana, the oppression of pure exhaustion mixed with insomnia infiltrated his DNA.

The cabbie pulled up to the curb and commenced to hauling Jasper's luggage into the trunk. Jasper sat in the back of the cab and noticed that the weather was something he could definitely get used to. The sun was much brighter than in Seattle, as if God had turned on the high beams. Even the roads were unusual—paved with coral and limestone.

"Eh, *hafa adai*. Where ya headed, brah?" the cabbie asked as he pulled out of the airport. There was a singsong cadence to his voice.

"I'm looking for a hotel. Any suggestions?" Jasper noticed in the back next to the window was a picture of the driver and his name in all caps: ANTHONY DELAROSA.

"Are you payin' or is it on the company's dime?"

"It's on my dime."

"I'da said the Hilton, but if you payin' outta pocket, I got the perfect place for ya. Very reasonable price and perfect view.

My cousin runs it. Just tell 'em the Antman sent ya and you'll get the family discount. Where ya from, brah?"

"Seattle. I'm looking up an old friend, a woman I dated many moons ago. Her name is Lani Sablan. She lives in Agana."

"Oh, my brutha, I hope ya not thinkin' a datin' 'er. The locals don't like it when boys from other villages come and steal their women, much less haoles from Seattle." He guffawed a resounding belly laugh. "What's her last name again?"

"Sablan."

"Ah, there lots of Sablans. Everybody related to everybody else in the Marianas."

"Do you know where I can buy some loco weed?" Jasper said.

Antman squinted at him in the rearview and laughed. "Ha. I know where you can get any-ting on this island, brutha. You jus' stick wit' Uncle Antman."

* * *

The Oceanfront Hotel wasn't directly on the beach as the name suggested, but it had a panoramic view from the sixth floor and was a lot cheaper than the luxury hotels. Antman gave Jasper his business card, and they arranged to meet the next morning to tour the island and track down one Lani Sablan. After knocking back a couple of aperitifs and eating grilled parrotfish in the hotel restaurant, Jasper retreated to his room and stared out the window at the water, at the ocean of possibilities. He tried to remember everything he could about Lani: how she loved stargazing and poetry, how she deflowered him in her sorority house, and her propensity to date independently wealthy frat rats far beyond Jasper's socioeconomic stratosphere. The anticipation was killing him, but he reminded himself, for good or bad, the nine years of wondering was almost over. Later in bed, he smiled as he drifted off to sleep, and the digital radio alarm clock played George Harrison's "Got My Mind Set on You."

The older Jasper got, the less he believed in accidents.

CHAPTER 5

SKYDIVING INTO THE VOLCANO

As the trade winds whistled through the jalousies and the white lace curtains waltzed to the persuasion of the tropical breeze, Jasper stood in his room observing the doves cooing in the palm trees and the sun glistening off the bluest of blue oceans. The suspense was agonizing. He had to call Lani now, to see if she even remembered him, to see if this pilgrimage was destined to be a pipe dream. No answer. He tried ten minutes later but still no answer. The lack of prescience was nearly palpable. Still, it was titillating to consider the possibilities—she could be standing in front of a window and gazing at the exact same landscape that Jasper was at this very moment.

* * *

The phone rang, the front desk informing him that Antman was waiting down in the lobby. Jasper hastily slipped slapdash into his cargo shorts, Emerald City Community College T-shirt, and flip-flops.

"Qué pasa, brutha?"

As they shook hands, Antman's meaty paw temporarily cut off the circulation in Jasper's fingers. He hadn't fully appraised Ant's size the day before, but today he noticed that his affable tour guide was the size of a small mountain. He was easily three hundred pounds, maybe three-fifty, with a bushy black beard, a dark complexion, and a polished clamshell necklace. His hair was piled into a tight bun in back, and several rogue strands, fine tendrils outlined by the sun, were refusing to capitulate. Jasper explained that no one answered at Lani's and could they just drive around to see the sights for a while?

"No problemo. And I found you some wicked weed, brah. My cousin who owns your hotel? He gotta a friend who gotta a friend, et cetera et cetera. He'll have it for you by lunchtime fo' sho'."

As they cruised from one end of the island to the other, Antman unraveled his personal narrative. He was from Oahu and moved to Guam a decade ago at sixteen when his parents decided to return to their roots. He once played varsity for the University of Guam's basketball team but tore his ACL. He had an ex-wife, a bachelor's degree in Pacific-Asian studies, two border collies named Heckle and Jeckle, and he'd been back to Hawaii only once. "I'm full-time Chamorro now, boss. One week away from dis place and I want to break shit and kill people. Ha."

Antman pointed out the indigenous flora and fauna, native birds like egrets and sandpipers, and various butterflies like the swallowtail and milkweed. Of all the landmarks, two were especially notable. There were cliffs where Japanese soldiers leapt to their death rather than face capture by the Americans in 1944. Also, along the same theme, there was another cliff called Two Lovers Point. Ant recounted the story with great drama and tonal inflection, gesticulating as if telling a child's bedtime story. Every so often, he would peer into the rearview to gauge Jasper's reaction.

"See that steep cliff? It overlooks Tumon Bay."

Jasper looked down the precipitous drop to the roaring waters crashing into the rocks over a hundred feet below.

"A long time ago when Spain ruled the land, a wealthy aristocrat married the daughter of a Chamorro chief. They owned land and were respected by both the Spanish and Chamorro. They had a daughter who was very beautiful and widely admired for her kindness and humility. She brought her family great honor and dignity."

"What was her name?"

"Shut up, brah. You killin' my mojo." Antman smiled into the rearview.

"Sorry."

"So anyway, where was I? Oh yeah, everyone admired her and shit, right? She was totally cool, yeah? One day, her father arranged for her to marry a Spanish captain, and she became so distraught that she ran from the capital to the north of Guam, where she found a secluded beach. There she met a handsome Chamorro warrior who was young and strong and from a modest Chamorro family. He was gentle, and his eyes searched nightly for meaning in the stars. Pretty poetic, huh, brah?

"Anyway, when the girl's father learned of the two lovers, he became completely crazy and insisted she marry the Spanish captain. That day at sundown, she met her Chamorro suitor on the shore. Her father found them, and his soldiers chased the lovers up that cliff above Tumon Bay."

Jasper looked out over the cliff. "Wow."

"The lovers were trapped between the edge of the cliff and the battalion of soldiers. When the warrior warned them to stop, the girl's father forced the soldiers to halt. The lovers proceeded to braid their hair into one long knot, looked deep into each other's eyes, and kissed one final time as if no one existed but the two of them. Then they leapt off the long cliff hand in hand and into the turbulent waves below. The father and all the soldiers rushed to the edge, but it was too late. The father stared at the water in pure anguish.

"Since that day, Chamorros have regarded the peak above Tumon Bay with great reverence. They believe that the two lovers are entwined there into eternity. And forever after, the high point on that cliff has been known as Two Lovers Point."

"Guam's version of Romeo and Juliet."

"Yup. Star-crossed lovers, Chamorro style."

* * *

After the tour, they went back to the hotel and ate shrimp salad in the restaurant. Jasper wanted a beer to soothe his nerves but also wanted to be sober if he met up with Lani. Antman excused himself and returned shortly with a smile. "I got ya stuff, brah. And I got a line on your girl, too, Miss Lani. My cuz says she lives in a big white house on da water, maybe a five-minute ride from here. I know right where it is, I even got the address. I think she rich, boss. I think she real rich. Her daddy was high up in the gov'mint. I never hearda him, but my cuz say he was big shit on dis island back in the day."

Rather than call her on the phone, Jasper decided to surprise Lani in person. His nerve endings were jangled again as he planned what he would say. More than anything, he was tired of the not knowing. Like a prisoner on death row, he had contemplated it long enough. If there was a firing squad, it was time to smoke that final cigarette and stare them in the eye. One way or the other. She loves me—she loves me not.

* * *

They drove to a nearby road that hugged the beach.

"Dis it, brutha. Not too bad, yeah?"

Jasper stared. It was the largest house in sight, a Spanish colonial with white columns and surrounding palm trees. The terra-cotta roof tiles stood in stark contrast to the dazzling white stucco. There was a small balcony on the second floor. The emerald-green lawn was postcard perfect.

"Wait here," Jasper said. "Keep the meter running." He strutted up the brick walkway like he owned it and felt himself breathing. Nine years and 5,663 miles had all come down to ten steps. There were tall windows with decorative black wrought iron trim. He took a deep breath and rapped the black door knocker three times. Dogs immediately barked inside. Just when he thought no one would answer, the door creaked open.

At first, he didn't recognize her. Her hair was short and flipped up in the back. She was emaciated: face sallow, cheeks hollow, and her eyes, her beautiful blue eyes, sunken and listless. She once told him she was the only native girl on Guam with blue eyes.

"Can I help you?" Three pit bulls were snarling menacingly behind her.

"Lani, it's me, Jasper. Jasper Trueblood. Remember back from Tucson, Arizona?"

She stared at him.

"Lani?"

"Shit," she said.

Jasper stood waiting. He knew it was really her, he could sense it, he just didn't know what to say. Clearly this whole thing was a very bad idea. After a protracted silence he said, "Remember this, Lani? *'Oh, do not ask, "what is it?" Let us go and make our visit. In the room the women come and go, talking of Michelangelo.'*" It was a line by T. S. Eliot, and he used to recite that poem in bed to her all the time. But this was not the same Lani. This was a bad imitation of the old Lani. Her complexion was pale. There was something wrong with her teeth. She had a faraway look in her eyes, even though she was staring directly at him. Jasper knew he had made a colossal mistake.

"You have to leave." She closed the massive door in his face.

Jasper stood for a moment, baffled and bewildered, completely confounded, thinking it might be a joke, but then he heard the dogs resume their cacophony of snarling growls. He had a flashback to when something similar happened almost a decade ago, naively showing up unannounced on his father's doorstep, finding his childhood home in utter ruins—the opposite of what he had expected. It was also the day his father revealed for the first time that Jasper was adopted. He waited a little longer on the doorstep, then walked shell-shocked out to the curb and ducked into the cab.

"Holy shit, boss. You no look so good."

"This was a mistake, Antman. That was a major tactical error. Let's get the fuck outta here."

Just as Ant shifted into gear and was about to pull away, someone came sprinting toward the rear of the cab.

"Stop, stop, stop," the woman shouted breathlessly. She slapped the fender and let herself into the back seat next to Jasper. "Drive," she said. "Anywhere. Just drive."

Antman pulled away.

Jasper was lost. "Who are you?"

"I'm Susan, Lani's sister. You talked to me on the phone a few weeks ago, right? Ring any bells? You're the poet. Don't ask me how, but she said three days ago that she knew you were coming. When you didn't call back, she said it was just like you to show up at the front door unannounced, and sure as shit and taxes, here you are. She even had a dream about you." Susan reached across the back seat of the cab, hugged Jasper hard like she wanted to crush him, and started crying.

Jasper was more confused than ever.

* * *

They pulled up to the Oceanfront Hotel and parked in back.

"I'll wait in the bar, brah," Antman said.

"Bullshit. You're coming with us. Don't worry, I'll pay for your time," Jasper said.

"No worries, haole boy. We off da clock now. Dis shit is gettin' good."

Susan looked a lot like Lani used to. She didn't have blue eyes, but she had the long silky black hair. She was wearing white tennis shorts and her hair was in pigtails. Also, like Lani, her hands were perfect. Magical. Surgical. Jasper couldn't explain it exactly. They hurried along toward the elevator, and Jasper unlocked the door to his room.

"I don't even know where to start," she said, sitting down on one of the beds. "Lani's married to this crazy fucking guy, Marcel Camacho. He was the reason she went to Arizona in the first place, to get away from his ass. Then when she came back home to help out with Dad, she got back together with him. He sells ice."

"Ice? You mean like blocks of ice?"

"No, I mean like speed. Methamphetamine. Glass, crystal, shard."

"Oh hell, brah." Antman stroked his beard. "Dat some serious shit."

"He has a friend who's a flight attendant for one of the airlines," Susan said. "She sneaks it in by the brick from the Philippines."

"Like cocaine?"

Susan explained that ice was like cocaine except it was cheaper, lasted longer, and you could basically mix it up in your kitchen sink. Marcel was very well connected. He was in bed with the local Guamanian police and known to move sizable quantities all over the islands, sometimes by canoe. "He gotta real bad temper, too," Susan said. "He loves to fight. When he's high, which is all the time, he drinks. When he drinks, he's liable to erupt like a volcano. He could blow at any time. That man is one crazy som bitch, ya know? Even if he just *saw* you with Lani, he might cut you up like shark bait."

"Fuuuck," Jasper said. "What have I gotten myself into?" It looked like he wouldn't be seeing any more of Miss Lani. He called room service and ordered some food and drinks. Ant broke out the weed and lit the pipe. They blew the smoke out the window, and Susan talked for twenty minutes about Lani and Marcel. "And she told me all about you. She calls you 'her poet.' She liked you. A whole lot. But you had your own shit goin' on."

There was a tap-tap-tap at the door. "Room service," Jasper said. He was suddenly famished. However, when he opened it, there stood Lani like a doll made of papier-mâché, next to a male companion who extended his hand.

"Hey, I'm Marcel. And you must be Jasper. I heard a lot about you, Professor. None of it good. Just kiddin'. Hey, can we come in?"

"Uh, sure," Jasper said. "This is my friend Anthony."

Antman stood up and shook his hand, then Lani's. Jasper noticed Lani didn't make eye contact, and Susan stopped, too. Their collective body language seemed to say *caution: proceed at your own risk.*

"This is my wife, Leilani. Smells like some good shit," Marcel said, nose in the air like a cadaver dog. Lani sat next to Susan on the bed. "I hope you don't mind we crashed your little party. Susan left in such a hurry, and a friend of mine who works here saw her pull up in a taxi, of all things. That was fucking odd, huh? Dontcha think? Why would my fucking sister-in-law be taking a fucking taxi to a fucking hotel less than a mile from her own house? Anyway, I thought she might need a lift home."

Susan rolled her eyes.

Lani was in cutoff jeans and a ruffled pink tank top. Marcel wore a white short-sleeved shirt, long camouflage pants, and he had his black hair slicked back. He removed a pair of Ray-Ban Aviators and slipped them into his shirt pocket.

"Anybody up for a little sumpin' stronger than the green?" Marcel sat at the table and crushed his Kool cigarette out in the ashtray. He opened up his wallet, unfolded a two-by-two-inch square cut from a high-gloss magazine, and dumped crystalline powder on the glass-top table. He reached into his boot, extracted a large bowie knife with a carved black handle, and removed the sheath. He placed a Mastercard on top of the powdery crystals and smashed them down with the silver butt end of the knife. Then he sectioned off some lines with the credit card and snorted one for each nostril. "Your turn, brah."

Jasper shook his head. "Uh, no thanks. I'll pass."

Marcel smiled his lunatic crocodile smile and laughed uproariously. "Ha! I knew it. You a fuckin' narc, brah? You look like a narc to me." He glanced back at Lani. "See, I told you. Your bitch professor is a fuckin' narc. The weed is just a front."

"I'm not a narc, come on, man. Here, I'll show ya." He did a couple short lines, which burned his sinuses like napalm. "Holy shit," he said. He tried not to stare at the knife. Jasper passed Marcel the pipe with the weed.

Antman, Susan, and Lani declined to join them.

"OK, more for us, eh, Professor?" Marcel smiled and did two more lines that were as long as pencils. "Don't mind if I do," he said.

Ant looked at his watch.

"So," Marcel said, "I wanted to invite you to a little Christmas get-together all the families are having on the beach tomorrow. You did know it was Christmas, right, haole boy?"

"Yeah, sure," Jasper said. "I'll go. I mean, why not?"

"Good. I'll come by early to pick you up. Be up by dawn. We need to go out to my farm and get the pig." He stood up and Lani stood up with him. "Come on, Susan."

"I'll walk home," she said.

"No, you won't. You'll get in the goddamn car." And as Marcel opened the door, room service appeared with a covered silver tray and ice bucket. "Have a nice lunch, Professor. See you tomorrow. Be ready by sunrise."

When all three of them had left, Jasper stared at Ant, and Ant shook his head.

"I wit' you, boss," he said. "Fuuuck."

CHAPTER 6

ROSE AND THE ROASTED PIG

It was Christmas morning when Jasper was jolted awake by pounding on the hotel door. He glanced at the clock radio: 6:43 a.m. He crawled out of bed and peeked out the peephole.

Marcel.

"Let's hit it, brah. You ready?"

Jasper wiped his eyes and got dressed. He took a hit of weed and offered some to Marcel.

"Don't mind if I do. You wanna do a couple rails?" Marcel was sniffling like he had a runny nose. Jasper noticed his arms and chest were chiseled. And it might have been some sort of a fashion statement, but his tennis shoes had laces that were untied, and it was causing Jasper an extreme case of cognitive dissonance.

"Man, thanks, but no thanks. That shit is too much for me. I had to take extra-strength Tylenol just to get to sleep. How come we're leaving so early?"

"We gotta cook the pig, brah."

They got into Marcel's black Corvette and were soon on a dirt road, which Jasper assumed was Guam's version of the outback.

"By the way," Jasper said, "merry Christmas."

"Yeah," Marcel replied without taking his eyes off the road.

They pulled into what Marcel must have meant by his "farm." It was nothing like the endless cornfields Jasper had grown up with in the farmlands of southern Illinois. There were three motorcycles, two cars, a pickup truck, and several men waiting. Most were wearing bandanas and sunglasses, a couple had barbed-wire tattoos around their biceps, a couple more were drinking Budweiser tall boys.

"See that back there?" Marcel said. "Behind that house? That's where I grow my ganja. You'll never see helicopters 'cause I got friends with the po-po. The cops know better than to mess with me. I own those motherfuckers. I own the Five-O on this island."

Jasper was quietly proud of himself for catching the reference to *Hawaii Five-O*.

Marcel pulled into the dirt field and parked. He high-fived his friends. One of them was dressed in a Santa suit. They said some things in what Jasper guessed was Chamorro and laughed a sinister laugh. One was smoking a bowl and handed it to Marcel. He took a hit and passed it to Jasper. "This is Leilani's haole friend from the States. He teaches at a college in Seattle." Marcel looked at him gravely. "I know that 'cause I traced the call you made seventeen days ago." Marcel cracked open a beer. "He's a poet."

The men laughed at this. One turned up the Christmas tunes on a boom box.

"Come on, brah. Let's say good morning to the little piggies."

Next to a corrugated tin shack and a massive banyan tree with twisted limbs was a slab of concrete encased by a chain-link fence. Inside the cage were three large pigs that, Jasper guessed, must have weighed at least 150 pounds apiece. A man with a long, braided ponytail opened the cage door and, after a few tries, lassoed a noose around one pig's neck.

Almost immediately, Jasper had a very bad feeling about this.

As the man dragged the pig out of the pen by his rope collar, the creature snorted, grunted, and dug his back feet into the dirt. Marcel walked over, kicked the pig's front legs out from under him with a wrestling move known as a leg sweep, and when the pig went down, the other men converged quickly and pinned it to the ground. It started to whine and cry as if it knew what was next.

Marcel trussed the pig around all fours with the rope. The pig squealed even louder. Then Marcel dragged it across the ground over to a large metal table, and several of the men hoisted the pig on top. It was wiggling and wriggling under the weight of the men's fierce grip, and one of them sprayed it down with a garden hose while another squirted it with dishwashing soap. They lathered the pig up until it was sudsy, and after rinsing it off, a couple of them took long knives and shaved the hair off the pig's back. Then they rinsed it again.

"Come here," Marcel said.

Jasper felt sick.

"Hold this bucket under its neck."

Jasper did as instructed and winced, sharing the porker's sense of impending doom.

"We waste nothing," Marcel said. "The guts are cleaned and mixed with the blood to make *fritada*, a kind of stew. My favorite part is the snout." He removed the bowie knife from his boot just as he had done in the hotel the day before. He cast a devilish glance Jasper's way and, with one swift motion, shoved the blade deep into the pig's jugular. The other men were suddenly silent as Marcel held it in there for a long time and twisted it with a grin. The pig fought and writhed, and when he tried to make one last break for it, some of the blood squirted out, partly on Jasper's shirt. Then the blood steadily streamed into the bucket like it was coming from a spigot.

Jasper pretended it didn't bother him, like he did this every day, but in reality, he felt sick and wanted to cry. He had never seen an animal die before, and one thing he knew for sure, he would never eat bacon again.

The pig's feet kept moving like he was trying to run away, a strategy that had no doubt served him well in the past, but then his feet moved less and less, and finally, the swine squinted directly and desperately at Jasper as if it knew he was the only one who could save him. Its eyes rolled back in its head and he stopped moving. There was blood all over the table and Marcel's arm, and it filled the bottom half of the bucket.

Jasper put the pail down and, amazingly, did not vomit. After considerable slicing and pulling, Marcel proceeded to behead the pig, and one of his accomplices shaved the snout and removed it. Meanwhile, the men flipped the pig on its back, and Marcel used his knife to remove the pig's balls and penis, which, again, was no simple task. He reached inside and wrestled out the esophagus, followed by the intestines, bladder, and entrails awash in blood. One of the men washed off the blood, urine, and feces with the garden hose, and stuffed the pig's gullet with stalks of lemongrass. Someone poured boiling water from a teakettle on the back of the carcass and used the straight razor to shave it once again. It was as if the pig had just stumbled onto some apocalyptic Orwellian *Animal Farm* barbershop. Marcel took his Bic lighter, burned the hairs off the pig's hooves, and then amputated them with a hacksaw.

"I'll save the pigs' feet for you," he said, sweating profusely.

"Much obliged," Jasper said.

"Feel good to get a little blood on ya hands?"

"Actually, I could use a drink."

All the men laughed.

* * *

Someone was rubbing the pig's carcass with herbs, but Jasper was no longer paying attention. He drank another beer and smoked more weed, staring off toward the nearest horizon. They stuck a length of pipe inside the pig's mouth and pushed it all the way through its gullet until it protruded out of its rear end. Then they rigged the pig onto a metal wheel that rotated it rotisserie-style. Underneath was a bed of bricks and hot charcoal that was slightly longer and wider than the pig. They sat on folding chairs, smoking, drinking, listening to more Christmas music, and speaking in Chamorro. Jasper had no idea what they were saying. Occasionally, one of the men would dip a mop in a bucket of hot peanut oil and baste old Porky up one side and down the other.

"Check this out, Professor." Marcel led Jasper and two of the men to a dilapidated building out back. Inside was a large ring with chicken-wire cages stacked on top of one another, each stocked with a colorful rooster. Marcel explained that the ring was called a cockpit, the roosters were called game-cocks, and cockfighting was the oldest sport in human history. He grabbed two of the roosters and held them tight in his arms like babies. He pushed their noses within inches of one another, tossed them up in the air, and stepped aside. "Check out this shit."

Jasper was not at all eager to watch another animal get killed. With every passing moment in the tropical paradise of Guam, he was reminded how much he was trespassing, an uncomfortable voyeur peeping through the bedroom window of a private island.

"Watch," Marcel said. "They're born to kill, but they need a little kick start." One of his compatriots fitted each bird with razor-sharp metal spurs that slipped onto the roosters' claws. Ribbons were tied around the ankles to hold the spurs in place.

The cocks squared off. They crowed, eyeballed and circled one another, heads bowed to the ground, beak to beak, two poultry prizefighters squawking and occasionally jumping into the air with flapping wings to intimidate the opponent. They lashed out with the razors, ducked, jabbed, and occasionally clipped the other bird in a frenzy of feathers and cock blood. Jasper felt himself getting nauseous again.

"OK, enough," Marcel said. His comrades removed the birds' spurs and placed the roosters back in their respective cages. "Tomorrow night they fight to the death. Tomorrow night you see a real cockfight, Professor," he said. "Maybe you make some money. This place'll be packed with at least thirty guys betting all their dough."

"Cool," Jasper said, thinking that hopefully by this time tomorrow night, he would be well on his way back home to Seattle. He needed to get the hell off Guam before Marcel mistook him for a barnyard animal.

* * *

Jasper drove with Marcel to the party site. Along the way, Marcel retrieved a small device about the size of a cigarette lighter from his pocket, opened a tiny valve, and sniffed hard from it with each nostril. He offered it to Jasper.

"Thanks, but no thanks."

Marcel killed his beer and tossed the can into the back seat. He reached behind him into the cooler, pulled out another can, and placed it between his legs. Jasper was thinking that, at this point, dying at the hands of a drunk driver might not be so bad.

"You not here to steal my wife, are ya, brah?"

Jasper laughed. "Of course not, Marcel. Why would you say that?"

"I say that 'cause I know you fucked her."

"Marcel," Jasper began, remembering what Lani's sister had said about his mercurial temper, trying to assuage him with whatever words in the English language he could string together that would get him out of this place in one piece. Diction plus syntax, don't fail me now, he thought. "It was a long time ago; we were all in college. People were hanging out and partying. Whatever may have happened back then is ancient history. Lani's just a friend, that's all. I'd never dream of trying to steal another man's wife. That would be fucked up. I would *never* do that."

Marcel suddenly turned toward Jasper and stared at him with eyes like the tips of those blades the men were using to shave the pig. Marcel stared long enough to make Jasper think the car might careen off the road. Then he turned back toward the steering wheel, guzzled his entire beer in one long swig, tossed it in the back with the rest of the empties, and cracked open another.

It was past two o'clock and the warmest weather Jasper had ever experienced on Christmas Day. They pulled up to the beach, and people were everywhere, sitting and standing under canvas tents so large that they might have once belonged to Ringling Bros. Lani approached, holding the hand of a pig-tailed little girl with a sippy cup, and both regarded Jasper with a kind of discreet caution reserved for a new animal at the zoo. Lani didn't say anything for a while and neither did Jasper.

"There are some people to introduce you to," she finally said. "First of all, this is Rosario. She's our daughter. Everyone calls her Rose."

Jasper, having had no idea a child was involved, did his best not to appear flabbergasted. He stooped down to make eye contact. "Hi, Rose."

She hid behind Lani's leg, then peeked out, blushing. "I'm three," she said.

"She mine, too, brah," Marcel said with a sardonic sneer. He took out his little plastic canister, sniffed into each nostril, and walked away with a trail of cigarette smoke in his wake.

CHAPTER 7

BLUE CHRISTMAS

Lani led Jasper around and introduced him to the in-laws, the outlaws, and finally to her parents, who both sported a shock of white hair and were extremely polite. Her father was bent over like a praying mantis and seemed especially frail. Lani instructed Jasper to bow and say "hafa adai."

Eventually, she led him over to the food tent, which was stocked with enough grub to feed the entire island. In the middle of one table was the newly arrived Porky, headless, its body pink and crisp, as well as several large fish with grill marks, shrimp, mussels, red rice, countless side dishes, and all the requisite accoutrements. One man stood with a dead palm frond to shoo away the flies that had managed to slip past the mosquito netting. Christmas carols played in the background. A priest perched next to a wooden manger, which contained a baby doll Jesus, said grace, and the feast began. Jasper had not said grace since his mother died. Back then, he wasn't allowed to even smell the food until grace was said, followed by the sign of the cross.

Jasper filled a plastic plate with a cornucopia of culinary delights, including a couple slices of old Porky with some barbecue sauce ladled on top (and a dollop of guilt on the side). He took a bite and felt slightly cannibalistic, though it was the most succulent meat he had ever tasted. He sat down with Lani and Rose and scarfed down his food while occasionally checking on Marcel, who was down by the shore with his friends, laughing and smoking, drinking beer and tossing a football. The majority of guests were dressed in formal clothes, and Lani explained the sartorial protocol. Most of them had just come directly from Christmas Mass, and no matter how hot or humid it was, it would be disrespectful to the elders to wear swimsuits on Christmas Day.

Under one tent were massive stacks of presents, and after everyone had eaten dessert and had their fill of wine and coffee, the children were allowed to tear into their gifts. While they eagerly ripped off the wrapping paper, Jasper noticed a black-and-white police cruiser off in the distance parking on the grass. Someone next to him said, "Free food. Must be the GPD." Someone else said, "To pass up free food would be a dereliction of duty." The officer, wearing mirrored sunglasses and dressed in plain clothes, smiled, and waved the *shaka*, an islander greeting with three middle fingers curled into a fist, pinky and thumb extended. He walked over to Marcel and slapped him on the back. Marcel reciprocated by fishing him out a beer from the cooler he'd been sitting on.

"Here," said Lani. She handed Jasper a small present.

He looked over to make sure Marcel wouldn't pounce on him. "I wish you wouldn't have," he said. "I shouldn't have come here. I'm sorry. I miss you. I've missed you ever since Tucson. I just wanted to surprise you. I didn't mean to complicate your life."

In her eye, there was a sparkle reminiscent of the old Lani, like a gleaming gold nugget in a miner's watery pan of silt. It was what remained of the Lani he'd once fallen for.

"Open it," she said.

"I didn't get you anything."

"That's all right. Open it."

Jasper unwrapped it, and inside was a Swatch, a colorful watch that was all the pop-fashion rage. It had a red band with a white face and blue hands. "Wow, it's cool. Thank you," he said. "Thank you very much." He wanted to hug her but didn't dare.

"I remember you used to work at Thyme Market. It's a kind of tribute to the old days."

"Thank you, Leilani."

"Please don't call me that."

"Lani," he whispered.

"I'm sorry about Troy Archer," she said. "I know the motorcycle accident was a long time ago, but I haven't seen you since it happened."

"Thanks." Troy was the lead singer of the iconic rock 'n' roll band the Unknowns that played Woodstock and sold out football stadiums. Jasper had accidentally met him at a bar in Tucson and was given backstage passes. The night he took Lani to the concert turned out to be the band's last live show. It was also the night he was deflowered at her sorority house. "Sometimes when I hear one of his songs on the radio," Jasper said, "I pull the car over to the shoulder and listen."

They shared a look, and then Rose in her periwinkle dress with white polka dots started to cry because a little boy had taken away her brand-new stuffed animal, which prompted Lani to exit midstream and address the crisis. Jasper fastened the watch on his wrist, then held it against his ear to hear the tick-tick-tick of the clock's mechanical heart. He looked over at

Marcel, who was pouring shots of Crown Royal for the cop and his other compatriots.

The sunset cast a sorbet spectrum of pinks and purples on the palette of the horizon and the bloated underbellies of passing clouds. Before nightfall descended completely, Lani's mother gathered all the children around for a rousing chorus of Christmas songs. Jasper was more than a little surprised when Marcel emerged with a saxophone and played a soulful brass accompaniment to "Silent Night." Some of the kids sang off-key, but Marcel was impeccably precise.

When they finished, the entire crowd clapped while Marcel shot Jasper a death stare that said, *try to take any of this away from me, and you'll wind up sleeping in the coral reef.* Jasper went for another beer.

Later, Rose was introducing Jasper to her new stuffed animal, a white bunny rabbit she had named Snowball.

"Did you know Snowball could talk?" Jasper asked.

It took some prodding on Lani's part, but Rose handed the rabbit over, and Jasper went into "Bosworth mode." It was harder to be a convincing ventriloquist without being able to manipulate the puppet's mouth, but Jasper had become remarkably adroit at speaking without moving his lips.

"Hi, Snowball. Can you say hello to Rose?"

"Hi, Rose. Thanks for naming me Snowball. I love that name. By the way, did you know that alligators have over three thousand teeth in the course of their lifetime? I'm not sure how many toothbrushes that would be . . ." Snowball rubbed his head against Rose's tummy, and it wasn't long before Jasper began to garner an audience just as he had on the plane. When he finished there was applause. He went to hit the restroom, a squat cinder block building near the parking area. When he finished, Lani's sister was waiting for him.

"Jasper. Dude. You're a pretty cool guy. I can see why my sister liked you and everything. But you need to get the hell outta here right now. I heard Marcel tell his friends that he's tired of seeing your faggot haole face. He's drunk and that's when the shit hits the fan. You need to leave like . . . *rapido*."

Jasper peeked around the corner and saw Marcel chastising Lani behind one of the tents. Susan instructed Jasper how to get back to the hotel—it wasn't too far, but he needed to leave immediately. Although intoxicated, Jasper was able to walk. "OK," he said. "Tell Lani I said goodbye. I was going to fly home tomorrow anyway."

"Here, this is from Lani." She handed him a piece of paper, a note folded in half. Susan hugged him and kissed him on the cheek the same way she had in the taxi the day before. As she walked away, he opened the note. It was more of Eliot's "Prufrock" poem.

> *I grow old . . . I grow old . . . I shall wear the bottom of my trousers rolled. Shall I part my hair behind? Do I dare to eat a peach? I shall wear white flannel trousers and walk upon the beach. I have heard the mermaids singing each to each.*

Jasper slipped out of the park undetected and without saying goodbye to Lani. He walked down the street, his spirit spread scattershot between the shadows and streetlights, under the canopy of mango and banana trees, star fruit and Spanish plums. He reread the note six times. Was it a warning? A distress signal? He had never felt so alone with so many people.

Past the trees and tourists, the stores and shops, Jasper continued to walk. He stopped by a church and stepped closer to read the plaque. It had been destroyed in a Japanese bombing raid during World War II and rebuilt by missionaries after the war. As he admired the ornate statue next to the plaque, he noticed a cop car driving at a crawl, followed by a black

Corvette. *Marcel!* The cop was shining a floodlight between buildings. Jasper hid behind the statue.

"Over der!" shouted someone from the 'Vette's passenger side. "The fuckin' haole over der." Both cars screeched to a halt, and Jasper ran behind the church. He heard voices gaining on him and darted down a back road that was wedged somewhere between Main Street and the salty surf.

Voices.

Footfalls.

He ran through a stretch of jungle, led by starlight, fear, and his jackhammer heart. He hid clandestinely behind a clump of trees and ferns, and when he thought the coast was clear, he headed out as surreptitiously as possible, praying to whatever saint was in that statue.

More voices.

More footfalls.

Across the street, there was a nightclub and a parking lot full of vehicles. He checked both ways, did not see the 'Vette or police cruiser, and made a break for the front door.

"Five dolla cover." Behind the man at the door was a sandwich board: Third Annual Drag Queen Christmas Bash.

"Excuse me? What's this place called?"

"The Hideaway. Five dolla cover."

Perfect name, Jasper thought. He handed the man a five-dollar bill and took one last peek behind him. Inside, onstage, six drag queens were prancing and strutting in short sequined gowns with scandalous décolletage, flamboyant wigs, a variety of hosiery, high heels, facial hair, and enough makeup for an industrial accident in a paint factory. There was one queen on the far left, the only one sans facial hair, who was absolutely stunning and looked as feminine as any woman Jasper had ever seen. Her bookend counterpart on the far right wore a Santa stocking cap with mistletoe attached to the top.

For the most part, the audience was dressed just as ostentatiously. Cheers, wolf whistles, and catcalls punctuated the music, which started with campy covers of Christmas classics such as "Deck the Halls" and featured a Rockettes-style synchronized high-step on "don we now our gay apparel."

Jasper hid in back by the bar among countless strands of tinsel and blinking Christmas lights. As inconspicuously as possible, he ordered a double rum and Diet Coke. Just when he thought he might be in the clear and that he had successfully dodged Lani's husband, in walked Marcel with his two mooks in tow.

"Shit," Jasper said. He hunted for a back door. Near the restrooms, he saw a pay phone. He ducked down and porpoised his way in that direction. He searched his wallet and found the business card of the only person on the island who could save him.

"Ant, Antman, it's me, Jasper Trueblood. The guy from Seattle? Ant, can you hear me? I know it's Christmas and everything, but I really need your help, dude. This fucking guy, Marcel, is going to stab me. If you don't help me, I swear to God, he's gonna pull that knife and gut me right here on Guam."

He had to ask Antman to repeat himself several times. The decibel level was deafening.

"I'm at a place called The Hideaway. I think it's a gay bar. I'm surrounded by drag queens. Marcel is seriously going to castrate me! Lani's sister even said so. Man, I don't wanna die. I gotta get off this island. Please, Ant, please. You gotta help me." Jasper stuck a finger into his free ear, the one that wasn't mashed into the phone. "I can jus' barely hear you. OK. OK. OK, thanks." Jasper checked his new Swatch. If he could blend into the scenery and slip out the back, Ant would pick him up in the alley in just a few minutes. As Jasper carefully, strategically periscoped his head up to take a last look around, Marcel made visual contact and locked on sight.

"Over der." Marcel was pointing Jasper's way as the music pulsed on with more yuletide carols.

I saw Mommy kissing Santa Claus underneath the mistletoe last night . . .

"Help!" Jasper shrieked to any queen who would listen. "Help! He's gonna kill me. Help!" Several of the patrons began to circle him. "He's got a knife. He's going to kill me. Help!"

The head drag queen stepped up front and center. He was enormous, even bigger than Ant, dark skinned, and wore a pink tutu with white leotards. On his head was a diamond-studded tiara. "Nobody gonna kill nobody. Dis my bar, and nobody killin' nobody in my bar. What da hell?"

Jasper pleaded, "I'm gay, OK? There I said it. I'm a homosexual. I'm queer and proud of it. I love dicks and I always have. Please leave me alone. I won't marry your sister. Please don't hurt me." Jasper was laying it on thick.

Marcel, fuming, with eyes heavily dilated, reached in his boot, and as he went for the knife, Jasper kicked into his ventriloquism skills. "I'll cut you, faggot bitches," he said without moving his lips. He pointed at Marcel's friend, the plainclothes cop. "Did you hear what he said? He wants to kill us. He wants to kill all of us."

The drag queens bum-rushed Marcel and his goons. In no time, the stage show had skidded to a screeching halt and complete chaos ensued. The houselights were up and the queens were kicking, throwing punches, and pushing over tables. Cocktail glasses crashed to the floor. Strands of Christmas lights were torn down and feather boas unfurled in the air. Confetti cannons sprayed fake snowflakes from the ceiling, and the entire scene resembled a bizarre, life-size snow globe. Someone yelled to call the cops. Someone else took a high-heeled shoe and started to pummel Marcel with it. Meanwhile, an Elvis Presley Christmas classic kicked in.

You'll be doin' all right with your Christmas of white,
but I'll have a blue, blue, blue, blue Christmas.

CHAPTER 8

MEET THE NEW YEAR, SAME AS THE OLD YEAR

"Psst, brah!"

Jasper was hiding in the alley behind The Hideaway waiting for Ant to pull up in the taxi, but, instead, he was driving a beige Chevy LUV truck. Jasper piled in. "Man, am I glad to see you."

Antman checked the rearview and did a quick U-turn. One police cruiser after another screeched to a stop in front of the club, lights whirring, sirens blaring. "They ten cop cars on da whole island, boss, and only five work on Christmas. Now they all here. What da hell happened in there?"

Jasper explained everything as they drove to the hotel, checked out, and went straight to the airport. He gave Antman the rest of his traveler's checks, $260 in all. "Here's my address," he said. "If you're ever in Seattle and think you can avoid breaking shit and killing people, you can stay with me and I'll take you out for the biggest steak you've ever eaten."

"You want me to get a message to Miss Lani?"

"Yeah," Jasper said. "Give her this." He returned the note with the T. S. Eliot poem. "Tell her she needs it more than I do."

Jasper gave him a bear hug and then waited as inconspicuously as possible in the airport, a baseball hat covering his eyes, newspaper in hand, afraid Marcel might materialize at any moment. He had this quixotic notion that Lani would show up and kiss him goodbye, but by takeoff early the next morning, the plane taxied down the runway with no Lani in sight.

As the aircraft passed over the international date line, Jasper went back in time and celebrated his second consecutive day of Christmas by sleeping all the way to Tokyo and halfway to Seattle. He also wrote a poem.

Directions to my island girlfriend

there's no street address
just look for the large hut
behind the clump of palms
next to the white beach
where Chamorro kids
drink beer & listen to hip hop
down the dirt road from the big market
(the fish market,
not the farmers' market)
then make a sharp right
ask around—you'll find it
if you've gone to the sacred
ancestral burial grounds
you've gone too far

The plane finally skidded to a landing on the tarmac. Jasper trudged into SeaTac Airport, relieved to be alive. He was profoundly grateful to feel the tiny pinpricks of drizzling rain and frosty welcome of forty-degree weather. He went directly for a pay phone. It was a call long overdue, one he could put off no longer, one that only the reprieve of a day in time had afforded him.

"Hey, Dad, it's me. Merry Christmas."

"Junior? Junior, is that you? Who is this?"

"It's your son." Then Jasper listened as his father scolded him. "Yeah, I know, I know, yes, it's been a long time. I know. I'm sorry, Dad." Jasper lowered his voice. "I said 'I'm sorry.' Look, let me explain." But there really wasn't much to explain. Yet again Jasper was reminded that truce or no truce, the war waged silently on. Could sons ever forgive the sins of the fathers? It was a delicate détente at best. For some reason, the bad memories still had more firepower than the . . . "Yes, Dad, I'm still here."

* * *

Relieved to resume his ordinary, quotidian life of monotony, conformity, and as Thoreau put it, quiet desperation, Jasper sat in the living room on the morning of New Year's Eve watching TV—"A Decade in Review"—as the occasional fish surfaced in the koi pond out the front window. He was writing a year-by-year reflection of the eighties that might someday become a series of poems.

1980: change name, escape to Tucson, turn twenty-one, drop out of school in three months, meet Troy Archer, meet Lani Sablan, find out I'm adopted.

1981: meet Connie (biological mother), bury Troy Archer, Iran hostages released, Reagan and Pope sidestep assassination.

1982: Troy's estate pays for me to finish undergrad.

1983: Cabbage Patch Kids, Connie wills me her house and IRA.

1984: George Orwell was right . . . about everything.

1985: grad school, famine in Ethiopia, hole in ozone, Rock Hudson dies of AIDS, *Titanic* found.

1986: space shuttle explodes, Chernobyl explodes, meet Daphne.

1987: finish grad school, DNA, Klaus Barbie, Black Monday, hired by Emerald City CC.

1988: will disco ever end? propose to Daphne.

1989: Berlin Wall, *Exxon Valdez*, Tiananmen Square, something called the World Wide Web, break up with Daphne, find Lani, nearly decapitated by Lani's psychotic husband.

Jasper was not sure where this series of poems was going, but it was interesting to think about how unpredictable the last decade had been and how equally capricious the next decade, a.k.a. his thirties, would be. He knew of a couple New Year's Eve parties that night but wasn't inclined to go. The dream vacation in Guam had siphoned the holiday spirit out of him like a sump pump. Nevertheless, there was one person he most assuredly did want to see. He smoked a joint, drove to the seedy side of Seattle, and parked under his favorite marquee: THANX FOR THE MAMMARIES!

Apparently, Ginger Snap was quite popular. Not only was the red light on at her booth, but there was also someone waiting outside the door. Jasper bided his time patiently until it was his turn, then sat down and shoved in forty dollars' worth of tokens. The shutter lifted and there she was behind the glass in all her glory. He picked up the red phone. "Hi, I don't know if you remember me. My name is Jasper."

Ginger's dreads were tied back, and she was wearing a midnight-blue baby doll negligee with matching G-string panties. She picked up her red phone. "Of course I remember you. I have a pornographic memory."

They both laughed.

"You visited me twice before Christmas. Now tell me what you want, sweet thing."

Jasper took off his jacket and made himself comfortable, but he did not undo his pants. She had the largest areolas and nipples he had ever seen. "Can we just talk, Ginger? I really need to just talk first."

"We can do anything you want, honey, as long as you brought enough tokens this time." She smiled.

He explained the saga of Daphne, of Lani, of how Antman had saved him from Marcel. After Jasper told her he was a professor at Emerald City Community College, he shared about his childhood growing up in Illinois. He described his life as a cocktail of equal parts boredom and bedlam, tedium and pandemonium, and said his favorite new word was *ennui*—that gnawing feeling of apathy and discontent. "Is anyone ever really happy in this crazy fucking world?"

"I'm happy with you right here, right now," she said.

"Can I ask what your real name is?"

"You can," Ginger said, "but it's against the rules for me to tell you."

"You have rules?"

She smiled and said in her sultriest voice, "We all have rules, Professor."

"What are your rules?"

"Damn, you really do wanna talk, don't you? Here, let me put you on speaker." She hung up the phone, slipped deftly into a white terry-cloth robe with the Ray's Pleasure Palace logo on the lapel, and suddenly there was a certain gravitas to her demeanor. "Do you mind if I eat lunch? I'm starving."

"Not at all," Jasper said. "Please do. What're you having?"

Ginger opened a wax-paper wrapper and began to eat a sandwich. "Mmm. Ham and cheese with bean sprouts and light mayo."

"Nice."

"So, here are my rules, Mr. Jasper," she said crossing her legs. "First, I never reveal anything about the real me—my name, where I live, what I do with my free time . . . That's all private. The thing is, though, men don't want to hear about all that shit anyway. They can get that at home from their nagging wives. What they really want is a sexy harlot to indulge their fantasies."

Jasper nodded. He had to admit that, at least up until this very minute, that was his story, too.

She took another bite. "This country is so sexually repressed it's ridiculous. Freud figured it out a long time ago. Freud said that the repression of sexuality is the key to psychoneuroses."

"He also said that sometimes a cigar is just a cigar."

Ginger Snap laughed. "That's true. Seriously, though, I blame it all on the Puritans. Sex is the most normal thing in the world—it's like breathing or sleeping, but repressed people wanna make it dirty and shameful. If you're unmarried but not a virgin, you're *impure*. If you have sex with someone other than your partner, you're *cheating*. And God forbid if you're female, just thinking about sex makes you *dirty*, makes you, quote, unquote, *a bad girl*. No wonder women are so neurotic. Women think about sex all the time. Women think about sex just as much as men do, but they're so afraid of their own bodies and their own carnal desires that they can't even function. Half of them are afraid to even masturbate."

"Damn Puritans."

"Damn straight, and you can thank 'em for those scarlet letters, too. Let me tell you something, Mr. Jasper. I've studied the human brain. Having lots of sex will virtually eliminate stress hormones from your brain chemistry. Lots of sex will make you live longer, healthier, and happier. On the other hand, a little sex is almost as bad as no sex at all. Minimal sex can actually stimulate stress hormones. By the way, do you know how to make a *hormone*?"

"No," Jasper said.

"Refuse to pay." Ginger Snap laughed. "I crack myself up sometimes. OK, here's another one. What did the left boob say to the right boob?"

"I give up."

"If you hang any lower, they're gonna think you're nuts." She laughed again.

"You're funny. I can tell you amuse the hell out of yourself."

"I should give myself some tokens."

"Ha," Jasper said. "You ever get female customers?"

"Occasionally, I'll get a couple of drunk sorority sisters. They're not supposed to, but I let them come in two at a time. I like women. I like everything about a woman's body. I'm bisexual as hell."

Suddenly, Jasper felt himself getting sparked. He invested the rest of his tokens.

"See, Mr. Jasper, here's the thing. Everyone is bisexual. For example, let's say you're a male heterosexual, which I assume you are. But think about it. When you watch porn movies, you don't want to see some guy with a flaccid little dick, do you? Hell no! You want to see a big hard penis. Get what I mean? Everyone's bisexual. It's just a matter of degree."

"I never thought of it that way."

"Freud also said that pure masculinity or pure femininity was not to be found in any biological or psychological sense."

"You kinda got a thing for Freud. Isn't he a little old for you?"

She twirled a dreadlock around her index finger. "Too much facial hair for my taste." She finished a carton of milk and wiped her mouth with a paper napkin. "Here's the difference between having sex with a man and having sex with a woman. Men are all about the act. Fuck and cum. That's it.

Even the good ones who understand the significance of fore-play really, down deep, jus' want to fuck and cum. Women are much different. Self-assured women are all about enjoying the pleasure of the touch. I've been with women when all we did was hold each other in bed all night. Fondle. Caress. Run our fingers along each other's erogenous zones. No pussy or ass involved."

"*Ass.* I'm glad you mentioned that. What's your position on anal?"

"Doggy-style." She laughed again. "No, seriously, every-body likes anal if it's done right. The problem is most men don't do it right. The trick is to never use lube. That's why the good Lord gave us saliva. You gotta use spit and you gotta take your time. That's the most important part. Lick it, finger it, fuck it, but take your time. It's not a fire drill."

"You ever let a guy cum in your mouth?"

"Of course I do. It's a good source of protein. Women who whine about it should just shut the fuck up and stop complain-ing all the time. I will grant you it's an acquired taste, all right? It all depends on the guy's diet. But if you can't handle it, hey, chase it with a nice merlot and stop bitching all the time."

Jasper pointed toward her mouth. "Oh, you got a little mayo on your chin."

Ginger wiped her mouth.

"Ha, gotcha!" Jasper said. "Just kidding."

"You're funny. You're my nutty professor. I like that." Ginger smiled and began twirling one of her dreads again. "You know, they say laughter is a form of consent. It means that intellectu-ally, I agree that what you said or did was humorous. It's a form of intimacy."

"Do you ever climax? I mean, when you're in here, do you ever have an orgasm?"

"No. Well, maybe a couple times, but it's pretty rare."

"OK, I have to ask this. Does size really matter to women? And be honest."

"Mr. Jasper, have you ever heard the old expression 'It's not the size of the ship but the motion on the ocean'?"

Jasper smiled. "And how long it takes for the *seamen* to disembark?"

"Ha," she said. "You have heard of it. Look, I'm not saying size is irrelevant, but the best sex I ever had was with a man who had a five-inch dick. I swear to God I never came so many times in my entire life as I did with that guy in one night. I literally almost passed out twice. Now, Professor, let me ask you a question. You ever been with a black woman before?"

"No," Jasper said. "But I heard a rumor that once you go black, you'll never go back."

"I started that rumor."

"Do you ever go out on dates? I mean, real dates? Like, with customers? I bet men ask you out all the time. I bet they wanna bust right through that glass."

"That they do, teach, that they do. Sometimes they beg. 'Please, baby, *pleeaasse*.' But I have never dated a customer, nor would I. You have to separate business from pleasure, even when pleasure *is* your business. And whenever I leave this place at the end of my shift, I always have two friends accompany me to the car: Mr. Smith and Mr. Wesson." She winked. "Just in case someone can't take no for an answer."

"Wow." Suddenly, Jasper wasn't so sparked anymore.

"One can never be too careful. A girl's got to protect herself. What else do you wanna know?"

"Do you like your job? I mean, you must get a rush from watching men masturbate, right?"

She paused. "Yeah, maybe a little too much. It's a power trip for sure. I admit I get off on it. I love to watch them ejaculate. They start hyperventilating and shaking, and I especially love to watch their faces contort when the money shot arrives.

It makes me feel a sense of . . . I don't know . . . vitality? The adrenaline is like a drug. The trick is, of course, to get them to spend all their tokens before they shoot their load. You don't want them to pop their cork prematurely, you know?"

"Yeah," Jasper said. "I found that out the hard way. No pun intended." He checked the timer: 05:58, 05:57, 05:56 . . .

"Striptease is an art. It's more about the tease than the strip. Pace, rhythm, timing."

"I like you," Jasper said. "You're smart. What other rules do you have?"

"Well, there are house rules, too. Legalities. For example, you see this finger? I can rub it against myself, but I can't put it inside myself. No digital penetration. And see this?" She took out a wooden box from behind her booth and opened it. Inside was an assortment of sex toys displayed on a red crushed-velvet liner: dildos, vibrators, french ticklers, and a riding crop. "I can do pretty much whatever I want with them as long as they don't end up inside me. That's the law. Believe it or not, a girl just got busted for that two nights ago."

"You're kidding. Seriously? What were cops doing here? They don't have anything better to do?"

"Hey, the vice squad is better here than in most cities. But yeah, they still come around. Direct descendants of those Puritans, I swear. Vice always works nights, which is why I prefer day shifts. Miss Ginger don't need to be traipsing around no jailhouse wearin' a damn thong." She winked. "Plus, I get more regular customers during the day. Men like you. They know me. I give them what they need."

"What's the craziest thing someone ever asked you to do?"

"Ooh." Ginger laughed. She winced and pursed her lips. "Most guys jus' wanna bust a nut, you know? Talk dirty to 'em and show 'em your titties. Some guys are these macho Machiavellian motherfuckers who want to degrade and humiliate you. And then there's the exact opposite—naughty little boys who want Mommy to degrade and humiliate them.

"My favorite is this one Englishman, a regular, an older gentleman, who wants me to speak like a Brit, *mate*," she continued in accent, "because the old ball and chain died just after they arrived here from bloody old England, and he kinda breaks my bleedin' heart. The old chap wants me to take down my *knickers* and show him my *arse* while he *wanks* off. He always wears these expensive Italian loafers. I guess you could say I got a thing for men who wear expensive shoes."

Jasper inadvertently tapped the toes of his New Balance sneakers.

"This one dude likes to tie a shoestring around his schlong until it's almost purple while I call him disgusting names. He's a super-freak. Another guy likes me to spit at him. Of course, then I have to clean the fucking glass when I'm done. But the craziest thing that ever happened? Are you sure you're ready for this? Are you sure you really want to know?"

Suddenly, Jasper wasn't so sure. Reluctantly, he nodded.

"You're not going to believe it. One day after my shift was over, the janitor came in to mop the floor and found a dead chicken!"

"Oh . . . my . . . God."

"Isn't that repulsive? I don't even want to know what that was all about," she said.

"I've got two minutes and thirty-two seconds left. What do you like most about sex? What's your favorite part?"

Ginger smiled. "The sexiest thing two people can do together is kiss. Don't get me wrong, I believe most of the world's problems can be cured with a good old-fashioned blow job. A little lipstick on the dipstick works wonders. But for my money, the most sensual act between two human beings has always been the kiss. There is nothing on earth sexier than a long, slow, lascivious, lust-filled kiss."

Jasper was staring at her, mesmerized.

"My other rules are pretty simple: I'm never late for work, never miss yoga class, never take street drugs, and I don't drink cheap wine. Life is too short for cheap wine. Oh, and I never wear an outfit more than once a month. My closet looks like Frederick's of Hollywood. I have so many bags of lingerie at home . . . I prolly got a good twenty grand invested in lacy underwear."

The timer showed 01:23.

"I wish I could find someone like you," Jasper said. "Someone who's sexy and smart and not a phony. Someone who's not all fucked up, y'know." Then Jasper had an idea. "Hey, I got somethin' for ya."

Into the phone, he seductively half sang, half whispered the greatest striptease song of all time.

"The minute you walked in the joint . . ."

Jasper did a quick hip shift and Ginger Snap started to laugh.

". . . I could tell you were a man of distinction, a real big spender . . ." Jasper didn't know all the words, so he hummed the tune into the phone as he turned the tide and stripped for his stripper. In the spirit of what's good for the goose is good for the gander, he slowly lowered his khakis, pulled down his white boxers with the red hearts, and danced as lasciviously as a good Catholic boy could.

Ginger Snap was now laughing so hysterically that tears were streaming down her cheeks and ruining her makeup. "Take it all off, bitch," she said and laughed some more.

At 00:00, when the black shutter began to descend, Ginger blew him a kiss, waved goodbye, winked. Jasper realized he had just spent forty dollars, and whether it was voyeurism, psychotherapy, or both, it was worth every tarnished token.

CHAPTER 9

FACADE

School started at Emerald City Community College along with the new decade, and Jasper inserted himself back into his unremarkable life based on work ethic and routine. He wowed his new ESL class with the mirth of the ever-jocular Bosworth, with whom Jasper had developed quite a reputation around campus. The vice president for Instruction even encouraged Jasper to apply for the full-time tenure-track position in the English department. Jasper's newest, favorite diction-related misstep of 1990 was from a young Mexican student named Ignacio. "The white rhinoceros is very meaningful to all the horny animals of Africa and Asia."

Three weeks into the new quarter, Jasper received a large manila envelope postmarked GUAM with an illegible return address. He shook it a little. A letter bomb from Marcel? He closed his eyes and, fearless to a fault, ripped it open. It contained a brief note from the Antman that read, *Howzit, brah?*

along with the front page of Guam's *Pacific Daily News* dated December 26, 1989.

Christmas Ball or Christmas Brawl?

Agana, Guam—Three men were arrested on Christmas night, including an off-duty police officer, at a private dance club known as The Hideaway on Marine View Drive, after a violent confrontation that included participants of the Third Annual Drag Queen Christmas Bash. Co-owner Echo Sanchez said, "The men who started the problems were outsiders looking to inflict harm on the gay community. One of the men had a knife and threatened to 'kill a *bakla*.' We're peaceful here. We don't want trouble, and hate crimes are not tolerated." Marcel Thomas Camacho was arrested for assault with a deadly weapon, violating parole, and possession of a controlled substance with intent to distribute. Guamanian police officials found four ounces of methamphetamine, a Schedule II federal narcotic, concealed in the console of his 1989 Chevrolet Corvette.

At the bottom of the page with a ballpoint pen, Ant had drawn a smiley face and written, *Next time you visit, remind me to get you a fake mustache!*

Jasper didn't think much more about Guam the rest of the school year. Then it was fall quarter after an uneventful summer. He had applied for, but did not receive, the tenure-track position in the English department. He was, however, one of three finalists, and the person who got the job had been in the department eleven years longer, so there was room for optimism. The intimation was to be patient, his time would come. The committee seemed especially impressed by his response to one question in particular.

"Why do you teach?"

In response, Jasper had shared an anecdote that occurred on the second day of the previous quarter, a day typically reserved for establishing classroom tone and attitude, part coach, part cheerleader. He discussed concepts of success like goal setting, visualization, and replacing negative self-talk with positive affirmations. At the lecture's conclusion, all the students filed out of the classroom except one—Yu Yan, a seventeen-year-old Chinese student who had been in the country for all of six days. She had straight black hair, black-rimmed glasses, and sat in the second seat, second row. (Jasper would later learn that in translation, "yu yan" was a description for a woman with a beautiful smile.) Jasper approached, expecting a question about the textbook or the syllabus.

"Do you have a question?"

She shook her head, then suddenly rushed into his arms while slightly convulsing and weeping a gut-wrenching sob. Jasper whispered, "Why are you crying?"

"Because," she said, her body still shaking, "this is the first time in my life I ever believed in myself."

"That," Jasper said, "is why I teach."

The committee members smiled in unison. One had a tear in his eye.

* * *

Jasper waded into a stack of narrative essays from his English 101 class on a Friday afternoon. The assignment was to write about a significant conflict in their life or in the life of someone close to them, how it was resolved, and the lesson learned. Jasper started with the story of Robert, an affluent white kid fresh out of a private, upper-middle-class high school, and his tale of righteous indignation aimed against his double-crossing, double-dealing parents who had promised him a new Nissan Pathfinder for graduation. Instead, they used the money to go on a Caribbean cruise. Robert was so incensed by the "act of treason and betrayal" that he had seriously considered burning down the entire house. As an alternative, he held wild parties every night and the cops were summoned on multiple occasions. Heirlooms were broken, a TV was thrown out of a second-story bedroom, and his two-timing parents would think twice before humiliating him again in front of his friends.

First world conflict.

The next essay was from a Cambodian woman named Lam. In the 1970s, her mother had been forced to witness Lam's father being beheaded in a rice field by the Khmer Rouge. The mother was threatened that if she cried, even a single tear, they would make her watch as they decapitated her children as well. Months later, the family starving, Lam's uncle organized an escape plan. Over thirty people piled onto a rickety fishing boat in the middle of the night, only the moon as their guide. Lam and her sister were instructed to rub maraschino-cherry sauce between their legs so if pirates tried to rape them, they would think the girls were on their menstrual cycle. The ploy worked for them but, regrettably, not for their mother, who was gang-raped right in front of them. The boat eventually capsized, and twenty-two friends and family members either drowned or died of dysentery. Lam, her sister, and her mother, somehow, miraculously, managed to survive.

Third world conflict.

A knock on the door startled him from his trance.

"Hi, Margaret," he said. "What's up?"

"I have a transfer call for you. Long distance. Are you busy?"

"No, not at all. Just grading papers. Go ahead and send it through. Thank you." A transfer call? Odd, he thought, since there was a direct line to his office. Then he heard the voice he had assumed he would never hear again, at least not in this lifetime.

"Jasper, it's me, Lani."

"Lani. *Lani!* Hi. When I called you last year, your husband traced the number. Is this smart to be calling me? Aren't you worried that he tapped the phone?"

"Marcel's in prison. Your friend Anthony got in touch with me. He explained what happened at The Hideaway that night. In addition to the initial charges, Marcel was later charged with attempted bribery, extortion, and witness tampering. Last week he was convicted and sentenced to five years."

"Shit, Lani, I am so sorry. I never meant for any of that to happen. Your sister told me to leave the barbecue 'cause he was getting psycho. I was walking back to my hotel when he and his friends chased me into that gay bar."

"It's not your fault. Marcel makes his own decisions. Listen, I need to talk to you about something else. Something serious. You got time?"

Jasper looked at his Swatch. "Of course, sure, but I was just on my way out. Let me call you from home. It'll be more private. I'll be there in twenty minutes."

* * *

Jasper rushed home, but before he called Lani, he torched a blunt the size of his thumb and poured a double rum and Diet Coke. In the back of his mind, as he dialed and then as Lani spoke, he kept thinking of Ginger Snap's catchphrase: *Tell me what you want.*

"I'll be honest with you," Lani said. "Back in Tucson, I wasn't the person you thought I was. I wasn't the person the sorority thought I was either. I was living a lie." There was a long hesitation. "You didn't fall in love with me, you fell in love with the idea of me. You fell in love with the person you thought I was, with the person you wanted me to be. But you didn't know the real me, because I didn't know the real me. No one did. Now I do, and I'm going to be straight with you. OK?"

"OK."

"Marcel and I have a very sordid history. We've been together since the eighth grade. His father was a dirty cop who was eventually brought up on corruption charges. The day before he went to court, Marcel turned fourteen and came home from school expecting a birthday party. Instead, he found his father hanging from an ironwood tree in the backyard."

Silence.

"Are you still there?"

"Yeah." Jasper stood at the picture window, staring down at the fish in the koi pond as they darted around and circled one another. "I'm here."

Lani went on to explain that Marcel was never the same. His sadness and shame turned to anger and hostility. He was violent. By the time he hit sixteen, he had been expelled from high school and was breaking into houses. He beat on Lani—a lot. She went to the University of Arizona to escape. She came back when her daddy had a heart attack. She hoped life with Marcel wouldn't be the same as it had been before, and it wasn't.

It was much worse.

"I became a prisoner in my own home. He threatened to kill me and kill himself if I ever left him again. I figured he'd kill me either way. Even now, with him in prison, I don't feel safe. What I'm about to tell you, I've never told anyone except Susan."

The phone connection wasn't great, but Jasper thought he detected crying. "Don't stop. Keep going."

"Jasper, I had two abortions. I did not want to bring a child into this world with a father who was so unstable. When I got back from Arizona, he was selling ice and associating with criminals. Some very dangerous people. I wanted to break away, but he would handcuff me to the kitchen table and whip me with a belt. I'm so afraid of him. Even in prison, he has ways of getting to me. And don't worry, this line isn't being traced. I made sure of that."

Jasper sighed. "That's good."

"Then, even though I was using birth control, I got pregnant a third time. I decided to have the baby. Rose. To this day, I'm still not sure whether it was the best decision or the worst decision I ever made, but I know I love her more than my own life."

"So, what are you going to do now?"

"That's why I called. I don't know why you came to Guam, but I have to assume it's because on some level, you still care about me. I love my island. I *am* my island. But I want to come back to the States. My father died last May, and Susan has plenty of help taking care of Mother. I was wondering if I could maybe come and stay with you for a while, just 'til I can get my feet on the ground. I want to waitress and finish school. Get my degree. I only have another year to complete my bachelor's."

"What about Rose?"

"She'd be coming with me."

"Oh." Jasper audibly inhaled and exhaled.

"I know this is a lot to absorb, Jasper Trueblood, and you don't have to answer me now. Take some time. I just want you to think about it. Rose and I don't need much, just a couch or an air mattress until I can afford a little place of our own.

I'm an emotional wreck, Jazz. My tropical depression evolved into an all-out typhoon. I need a new start. Rose does, too. I've never been to Seattle, but I hear it's beautiful."

"It is."

"And I haven't used ice or any other drug since the night Marcel was arrested. I'm done with all that for good, you have my word. So . . . will you think about it? Can I call you in a couple days?"

"No," Jasper said. "Don't bother. There's no need to call. I want you to come. Rose, too. I have room, so stay as long as you want. But aren't you concerned about how Marcel will react when he finds out? You said yourself he still scares you."

"I have to do this, Jasper. I have to do it for myself and my daughter. I can't live the rest of my life in fear. Susan says fear is an acronym that means one of two things—*face everything and recover* or *fuck everything and run*. I'm not sure which this is, maybe a little of both, but you don't have to worry about Marcel. He thinks Rose and I moved to Fiji to live with my friend Cicely. It'll take a few weeks to make the arrangements, so I'll be in touch. And Jazz—"

"Yes?"

"I love you for this."

* * *

The next day, when Jasper realized it hadn't all been a damsel-in-distress dream, that Lani and her daughter were actually in real life coming to live with him, he panicked. He didn't know a damn thing about little girls, big girls, medium-sized girls, or any other girls. He recalled one of Ginger Snap's favorite quotes from Oscar Wilde, "Women are meant to be loved, not to be understood."

He arranged the house so they had their own space, a little privacy. What was once his office was now the spare bedroom.

He wondered if he was still in love with Lani or the idea of her or any other part of her. Where did infatuation end and love begin? What was the boundary line, the perimeter? When it came to the topic of love, the only definition everyone could agree on was that it was the score of zero in tennis.

* * *

The next morning Jasper fired up a joint, drove out to his therapist, and loaded the coin slot with twenty dollars' worth of tokens. The shutter rose.

"Well, if it isn't my favorite educator," she said from behind the glass. "I haven't seen you in a minute, Professor." Then, after Jasper sat down, she said in her sexiest whisper, "Tell me what you want." She was wearing her indelible smile, a peach-colored peekaboo bra, matching G-string, and the gold cross necklace. Her eyelashes were amazing, lipstick candy-apple red.

"I like that shade of lipstick. It makes a statement."

"Yeah? What does it say?"

"Well, it sorta says two things. First, I want to fuck you. Second, I want to kill you."

Ginger Snap laughed her irresistible laugh. "They don't call me 'the black widow' for nothing. Actually, I'm more like a brown recluse. So, come on, Professor. Tell me what you want. What is it that brings you in to see your mama today?"

"I want everything you got. I'm horny as fuck, and I want you to make me forget about every damn thing outside of this booth. I want you to make me forget about the entire planet and civilization. I want you to make me forget every single human being who occupies it. I wanna see penetration."

She blushed. "You know I can't do that."

"Bullshit. You can do it for me. I mean, you seriously think I'm the vice squad? Come on, baby, I told you I teach at Emerald

City. I told you about my childhood. I told you all about me. I know all about your rules, but I want to watch *you* have an orgasm. You said this shit makes you feel powerful, so make *me* feel powerful." In almost no time, Jasper was as hard as an Idaho potato. He tapped against the glass and said into the red phone, "I want you to break the rules. I want you to make an exception. I want you to let me in a little."

"You know I can't do that, Professor, but I think I can help you get to where you want to be." She pulled out her box of toys.

It wasn't long before Jasper shot his load all over the floor, his heart pounding wildly. When the shutter descended, he went out into the arcade and purchased another twenty dollars' worth of tokens. Her light was on, so he had to wait for the next c.o.p. to exit.

"You're back for more? I'm impressed."

"Aren't you going to say, 'Tell me what you want'?"

"I thought you already got what you want."

"I did," Jasper said. "But now I want something else."

"OK, have it your way. Tell me what you want."

"I want to talk to you as a person, as a real person. I know I don't really know you. I know you're playing a role and all that shit, right? A facade. I know all that. You told me all that. But you always say, 'Tell me what you want.' What I want is advice. Real advice from a real person." Jasper could see his reflection in the Plexiglas.

Ginger slipped on her white robe and turned down the techno music. She smiled. "Talk to me, teach."

"The girl from Guam? The one I went to see last Christmas, with the husband who is one crazy motherfucker?" Jasper told her about Marcel being arrested and convicted. "Last December, Lani was still using, right along with Marcel. She didn't look anything like she did back in college. I mean, not even close. And now that her husband's locked up, she wants to come live with me and bring her kid, too. She says she's been clean ever since he got arrested. That was the night I left Guam. That was over nine months ago."

"Are you in love with this woman?"

"See, that's the thing. That's the whole conundrum in a nutshell, isn't it? I'm not sure what I am. She says that back in college, I didn't really know her. She says I didn't fall in love with her, I fell in love with the *idea* of her. What does that even mean—I fell in love with the *idea* of her?"

Ginger Snap sat back, hung up her red phone, and put him on speaker. "That all depends. What was your *idea* of her?"

"That she had honey-colored skin and was exotic and erotic as hell. She was from a faraway land and loved poetry. She had beautiful hands. And even though I was broke, she didn't seem to mind. There was something special about her. The first time I was with her, I remember thinking I could see myself marrying this girl."

"And she was your first lover?"

"How did you know that?"

"You told me a long time ago. Was she good in bed?"

"Yes. I mean, I didn't have anything to compare it to, but . . ." He nodded and smiled. "Yes."

"OK, but think about it. Were you in love with her because of who she really was, or did you just want a piece of ass?"

Jasper considered it. "No, I didn't just want a piece of ass. I wanted the whole ass. The complete ass in its entirety."

Ginger Snap laughed. "Come on, seriously, did you love her? Were you in love with this woman?"

"See, that's the thing. I really don't know. I honestly don't know the answer to that. My mother had just died. I changed my name and left my father without telling him where I was going because I hated him so much. By the time I met Lani, I was lost. So, I don't know. I . . . don't . . . know. What more can I say?"

"You don't have to say anything. 'I don't know' is a complete sentence all by itself."

Jasper checked the clock. His time was almost up: 00:17, 00:16, 00:15 . . . "I do know one thing. I'm in love with you."

"Ha." She laughed. "You're not in love with me." She was smiling and twisting her dreads. "You're just in love with the idea of me."

CHAPTER 10

RECONNAISSANCE

One thing Jasper had learned incontrovertibly about teaching at a community college—the job was never finished. There was always a new lecture to plan, more papers to grade, another test to manufacture . . . Sometimes just coming up with the alternative responses to multiple-choice questions gave him the biggest headache.

Two days after Thanksgiving, Jasper was waiting patiently at SeaTac Airport for the long-anticipated arrival of Lani and her daughter. It was partly surreal, partly ethereal—both ridiculous and sublime. A decade ago, he never would have imagined this day was possible, that he would actually be living with Lani Sablan. And while there was a bona fide euphoria attached to that fact, firmly embedded in his brain like a tumor was the knowledge that even though technically Lani had been liberated from Marcel physically if not legally, and even though he was incarcerated with no custody or visitation rights, he was still capable of storming the Bastille at a moment's notice.

Jasper knew he would never feel completely safe so long as he and Marcel were sharing the same planet. Still, to think he would someday be living with Lani Sablan from the island of Guam, platonically or otherwise, was like living in a lucid dream.

Unable to sleep, he had arrived at the airport five hours early. To occupy himself, he graded English 101 essays. He was never sure if his students' compositions were fact or fiction, but as long as they were interesting, he didn't really care. One of the best pieces he'd ever read was by a student named Chase.

Because Chase sat, rather reclusively, in the back of the class next to the windows, Jasper assumed he was introverted or at least a little on the shy side. Nevertheless, no matter the topic, whenever called upon, Chase would push his black-framed glasses up on his nose with his index finger and share something insightful and often ingenious. He often perceived subtle details of the prescribed text that even Jasper had not considered. Chase consistently elevated the intellectual dis-course, and Jasper could only hope the students were learning as much from him as he was from them, especially the go-to students like Chase.

In his most recent essay, Chase wakes up one Saturday morning, makes a cup of hazelnut coffee, and decides to visit his mother in Tacoma. He is driving his Subaru along the interstate when the car in front of him attempts a sudden lane change, zigs when it should have zagged, and broadsides a black sedan. As it attempts to correct itself, it overcompensates and completely loses control. Chase hits his brakes and watches in horror as the car careens down the shoulder and flips 360 into a ravine. Chase pulls off the highway immediately and rushes to render aid.

The Latina driver has been thrown through the windshield of the vehicle and lands several yards away. Her face is badly cut, blood drips from her nose, and her arm is bent back in such a way that her left forearm is protruding through the skin. Chase is a certified nursing assistant and knows this is a compound fracture. He does not dare move her. Other vehicles pull over as well. The driver of an eighteen-wheeler approaches. "I just called it in," he says. "An ambulance is on the way."

Chase lies down in the wet grass next to her.

"I going to die," she whispers.

"Like hell you are," Chase whispers. "I won't let you die."

They exchange a shared look of confusion, of longing, a lingering look that says nothing and everything simultaneously, a look saying that for some unknown reason the gods have inexplicably fated these two strangers together at this place and time in the universe and right now, all they have is each other. The only question is whether that will be enough.

"Don't move," Chase says. "An ambulance will be here any minute."

Her eyes begin to roll back in her head.

"Hey, hey, hey," Chase says. "What's your name? Tell me your name."

"I going to die."

"There's absolutely no way I'll let you die. You have my word. Now please, tell me your name."

"Lu-cin-da." Her eyes start to close again.

"Lucinda, Lucinda, stay with me. They're coming to get you, but you have to stay awake. Where are you from, Lucinda?"

"I never got marry," she whispers. "I die now but never marry. I just want to love someone and get marry."

Chase was eye to eye with her now, mere inches from her face. "I'll marry you, Lucinda. I want to marry you." She begins to shiver. Chase removes his denim jacket, gently wipes the blood from her face, then carefully places the jacket on top of her. "I want to marry you, Lucinda, but you have to stay awake."

"You sweet," she says. "But you no mean it."

"Oh, believe me, if I say it, I mean it. You don't know me, but that's just the way I am. My name is Chase, and if I say something, I mean it. I swear I do. Lucinda, will you please marry me?"

There is a trace of a smile on her tender, broken face.

"Yes," she says. "I marry you, Chase."

He removes his pinky ring and slides it delicately on her ring finger. There is a second trace of a smile.

When the state patrol and EMTs arrive, she is placed on a gurney and rushed downtown to Harborview Medical Center, the most advanced trauma unit in the Northwest. Chase follows them, and when they pull into the ER entrance, it seems to take an eternity to extract her from the ambulance. Why is it taking so long? Chase wonders. As he parks his car and approaches, he sees why. The sheet has been pulled up over her head.

Jasper could feel himself tearing up as he tapped his red pen.

* * *

As Jasper scanned the passing faces like an advance scout on a reconnaissance mission, he finally found the faces belonging to Lani and her daughter. He waved and Lani waved back. This is it, Jasper thought. This is it.

It wasn't nearly as awkward a moment as Jasper had expected. He had already decided to give them as much space as they needed. She would be staying as a guest, as an old friend, and he did not pretend to assume any more than that. He handed her a bouquet of flowers and they hugged briefly. He crouched down to say hello to Rose, who was hiding behind Lani's legs.

"I see you back there, Miss Rose. You remember me?" She was wearing a pink taffeta dress and a pink beret to match. Lani wore jeans, a white long-sleeved shirt, and her hair was tied into a ponytail. She looked a lot less gaunt than the Lani he saw on Guam and a lot more like the Lani he remembered from college.

"Getting through customs took forever," she said. "Thank you again for doing this."

Jasper smiled and pushed the cart carrying their three large suitcases toward the parking garage. "I'm sorry," he said. "I forgot to buy a car seat."

"That's OK, I'll sit in back with her."

On the way out of the airport, Rose fell asleep and Lani talked about plans for the future. The first order of business was to get a waitressing job and save enough money for an apartment. After that, she intended to go back to school and complete her degree. Ultimately, she wanted a master's degree in social work, and Jasper presumed this was to help those who had been through what she had been through. The Lani he remembered was highly proficient at empathy and compassion, at ethos, pathos, and Logos, at least for others if not always herself.

Jasper looked at her through the rearview mirror; her hair was longer now, and her face was framed rather angelically by the sunlight slanting through the windows. "You look great," he said.

"Thanks, you too. And thanks again for doing this, Jazz. Remember when I used to call you that all the time back in the day?" She continued, "I want you to know this up front—I'll never do ice again. That poison destroyed me and ruined Rose's father." She paused. "To be honest, there were times when I wished you were Rose's father."

Jasper paused in kind. "I'm glad you're here."

"Recite some poetry for me? Like the old days?"

Jasper smiled and kicked into a schmaltzy old favorite by Pablo Neruda, and he used his old-time poet voice that was similar to Winston Churchill's.

I love you without knowing how, or when, or from where. I love you simply, without problems or pride: I love you in this way because I do not know any other way of loving but this, in which there is no I or you, so intimate that your hand upon my chest is my hand, so intimate that when I fall asleep your eyes close.

Jasper glanced again into the rearview. She was wiping her eyes. He could already feel himself falling for her all over again. And he could swear it was her, not the idea of her. He slipped his hand back between the seats and she held it. He asked if she was too exhausted to do some quick shopping.

"No, I'm fine."

They bought groceries and a car seat for Rose, then stopped by McDonald's because Rose was awake and apparently in need of a Happy Meal. By the time they coasted into Jasper's driveway it was nearly nightfall, and none other than Mrs. McCready stepped out of her house carrying a honey-baked ham with slices of pineapple toothpicked to the top. She hugged all three of them, and as Jasper retrieved the luggage, Rose noticed the koi pond. "Fishies! I see fishies!"

* * *

Jasper had successfully transformed his office into a bedroom for Lani and Rose with an empty closet for their clothes, sheer white curtains on the window, and a queen-size inflatable mattress with sheets, blankets, and pillows. On the walls were large cutout figures of *Sesame Street* characters he had found at the Goodwill store. He led his guests on a brief tour, and after Lani gave Rose a bath, they all settled in on the couch, ate three-cheese pizza, and watched *The Wizard of Oz* on TV. Rose was soon fast asleep, and when Lani yawned, she and Jasper bade one another good night. Lani gave Jasper another hug, more demonstrative than the one in the airport. "Good night," she said as they exchanged a glance that Jasper would later try to decipher for any hidden symbolism, intended or not.

He lay in his bed and reflected, reminisced, speculated. Whatever his life had been up to now, it would never be the same. Hours later, there was a delicate knock at his bedroom door. "Come in," he said.

Rose was holding the same stuffed bunny rabbit she had received that Christmas on Guam, although now it was soiled and had an eye missing.

"Are you OK?" he asked.

"Are you my new daddy?" she said.

Lani stumbled in rubbing her eyes and wearing an oversize I LOVE GUAM T-shirt. "Honey, we talked about this. Daddy got sick and had to go away for a while. Jasper is your friend."

"Oh," she said matter-of-factly. She climbed up on Jasper's bed and sat down next to him. "My grandpa is in heaven with Jesus. He died."

"Why don't you two come in here and sleep with me?" Jasper said. "It's a king-size bed and there's plenty of room. Plus, Rose, I have something to show you." He fetched Bosworth out of the closet. "This is Bosworth."

"Hi, Rose. Hi, Snowball," Bosworth said. "I think we're gonna be gooood friends. Can I sing you a song?"

Rose looked over at Lani, who nodded, so Bosworth really laid on the cheese.

> *My wild Irish Rose, the sweetest flower that grows, you may search everywhere, but none can compare with my wild Irish Rose. My wild Irish Rose . . .*

They all went to sleep in the same bed and the next morning ate blueberry pancakes with maple syrup. After that, Lani talked him into doing something he thought he'd never do again—go to church. They went to the nearby Catholic church for Mass, and it seemed like the Great Spirit in the Sky might be back on Jasper's side. He even sang along with the hymns. Then it hit him: for the first time in a long time, he was happy. Really happy. That night, when Rose dozed off, Jasper and Lani made love for the first time since Tucson, now over a decade ago, which they subsequently proceeded to do often when Rose went to sleep.

They decorated the house and spent Christmas together and read poetry in bed, sometimes with Rose and Snowball. Mrs. McCready brought over her famous cranberry bread. Life was like a Norman Rockwell painting, and Jasper wondered how long this lucky streak could last. Occasionally, Rose would hand him her toy telephone. "It's for you." And, of course, he would answer it. Sometimes Bosworth answered it, too. But the best thing about Rose was when Jasper returned from work, every day without fail, Rose would run up to him, hug him, and say the exact same words: "You'll never guess what happened to me today." It was always the highlight of Jasper's day. At night, he read her nursery rhymes. There was electricity inside her small spirit that spread like heat lightning.

Surrounded by all this contentment, Jasper decided this wasn't a lucky streak at all. In fact, he decided he no longer believed in luck. He believed in hope. He felt hope coursing through his veins as never before. Still, similar to the brilliant student with the potential to make straight A's but a penchant for procrastination and self-sabotage, Jasper had always tended to be more afraid of success than failure. There was a nagging voice in the back of his head saying, *"Don't screw this up."*

CHAPTER 11

A LINE OF DEMARCATION

By the time school restarted in January 1991, Lani had already secured a waitressing job at a high-end steak house downtown in Pioneer Square where, counting tips, she made more money than Jasper. He got used to having Rose's toys scattered on the floor and Lani's pantyhose hanging off the shower rod. Rose was resistant at first to her new day care arrangement, a licensed professional recommended by Mrs. McCready, but when she discovered other kids to play with, she was all in. Now she was the first one out of bed. One morning, Jasper walked out to the living room and found her trying to open the ground-level window so she could "swim with the fishies."

"No, honey, don't do that. You'll scare the fish." He had to remember to solder that thing shut.

On the weekends, the three of them played the tourist game: hikes, top of the Space Needle, elephants at the zoo, sharks at the aquarium, and flying fish at Pike Place Market. They did all the things that out-of-towners do, and native

Seattleites tend to take for granted. They navigated a paddle-boat on Green Lake and even took a drive one Sunday after church all the way up to Mount Rainier. Lani put a down payment on a car, so she was no longer at the mercy of the Metro schedule and waiting at bus stops in the rain. Rose asked why it rained so much, and Jasper explained that sometimes the world got sad and had to let it all out.

"Oh," she said matter-of-factly as if she had suspected this all along.

Lani seemed to understand that there were times when Jasper needed to stay in his office at school and grade papers, and he understood, too, that occasionally Lani needed to be wined and dined. Mrs. McCready was always happy to babysit. Jasper and Lani even left little yellow Post-it notes for each other on the bathroom mirror and the refrigerator, some with arrow-pierced hearts.

I love you.

I love you more.

Sometimes they lit candles and had romantic late-night dinner dates in the kitchen after Rose went to sleep.

One day, Lani came home from work and made supper—pork chops with scalloped potatoes—and put Rose to bed early. Rose, who was sleeping all by herself now in her big-girl bed, was engulfed by stuffed toys and, of course, Snowball. Lani had officially moved into the master bedroom with Jasper. After dinner, Jasper was grading papers in the living room and intermittently watching *Monday Night Football* while Lani relaxed in the leather recliner and emptied the pockets of her work smock on the coffee table.

"Holy shit," she said.

"What?" Jasper said.

"Ho-ly shit. Look at this." She picked up the tiny tied-off corner of a cellophane bag containing a sparkling white powder and held it in the air.

Jasper's eyes widened. "Is that what I think it is?"

"Dammit," Lani said. "These crazy guys from the radio station come in every day for lunch, and one of the DJs must have slipped it into my pocket. They're always joking about skiing the slopes with Frosty the Snowman."

Jasper untied the bag and sniffed it. "This isn't ice, is it?"

"It's definitely cocaine, but no matter what it is, I don't want any of it. Here"—she held out her palm—"let me flush it."

"Hey, if it's not ice, what's the harm? Now wait just a minute before you flush that," Jasper said. "Do you mind if I try it out? Just a little? I mean, I know your past, and I'm not asking you to do any, but I still like to party. *Please?*"

"I'd rather flush it," she said. "And I'm really pissed off at those guys. What would've happened if I would've gotten pulled over by a cop for speeding or if Rose would have found it?"

Jasper tried to imagine flushing it down the commode but couldn't. "The only time I did coke was on a float trip five or six summers ago, and it was cut so much that I didn't even get off. Come on, Lani. Just this once?"

Lani scooped the rest of the contents back into her purse: sunglasses, makeup, a handful of cash from tips, paper clips, bobby pins, and tissues. "Suit yourself. I'm going to bed," she said.

After she closed the bedroom door with considerably more force than necessary, Jasper was tempted to do as she suggested and flush it. In an instant it would be gone forever. But he didn't. Instead, he chopped it up with a credit card and laid out a few lines. He snorted two, then two more and then rubbed it on his gums inside his upper and lower lip. Wow, this was nothing like the speed-laced stuff on the float trip that made him do nothing but grind his teeth all night. He did two more lines and looked at himself in the bathroom mirror. His eyes were wildly dilated. He sat back down and rubbed his tongue against his gums.

Lani opened the bedroom door and without physically emerging shouted, "Don't forget you have class in the morning!"

Jasper sat up by himself all night, snorting line after line until his nose was so wrecked that he had to drip some water into his nostrils and sniff hard to clear his nasal passages. By six in the morning, the coke was all gone. He licked the inside of the bag and was watching *Sesame Street* on TV when Rose wandered out of her room.

"Hey, little girl."

"You look funny."

Jasper put the bag in his pocket and made her a bowl of Frosted Flakes, played airplane with the spoon while feeding her one bite at a time, and sang "The Yellow Rose of Texas" in a deep baritone. He felt absolutely amazing. Every cell of his body seemed to snap, crackle, and pop. Now he knew why people loved this drug. He never felt so alive, so aware—almost like he could fly! Life was instantly and infinitely better with it than without it. In a few short hours, cocaine had become his new best friend. Even reading *USA Today* became an excursion into the unknown.

"Are you my daddy?" she asked for the hundredth time.

"No, baby, I'm your friend. Bosworth is your daddy."

With a theatrical flourish, Rose placed her little fists on her little hips. "He not my daddy. My daddy sick."

* * *

Jasper wasn't sure he'd make it through classes, but miraculously, by the end of the day, he was still standing like a punch-drunk prizefighter.

"Are you all right, sir?" asked one student.

"Yeah," Jasper said, sniffling almost constantly. "I think I'm just fighting off the flu."

Back in his office, he called Christopher. "Hey, bro, I need a couple of tickets."

"What time?"

"Three thirty."

Jasper drove extra carefully, feeling the weight of his drug-induced insomnia. As he walked up to Christopher's condominium, someone he had never seen before was exiting. They avoided direct eye contact. He rang the doorbell. Christopher appeared and immediately went into his ritual.

"Hey, can I ask you a question?" Jasper said.

"Sure."

"You know I have that new girlfriend, right? I told you about her coming from Guam."

"Yeah." Christopher was weighing out the buds.

"Well, she's got a bit of a hankering for some blow. You know where I can get some?"

Christopher stopped midmotion, wide eyed like he'd just been bitten by a cobra. It was the first time he made eye contact. "You mean like cocaine?"

"Uh-huh."

He smiled and shook his head. "Nope. I don't touch that stuff anymore."

"Do you know anybody who does?"

Christopher turned away and finished weighing the weed on his high-tech digital scale.

"It's not for me," Jasper lied. "It's for Lani. Just a little. Just this once."

Christopher wrote down a number on a piece of notepaper. "This is his pager. He'll have to meet you first. He's paranoid as hell, even worse than me. That's what coke does to you."

"What's his name?"

"T-Bone." Christopher handed Jasper the bag of weed and counted out the ninety-five dollars one bill at a time. "Sit down," he said.

Jasper checked his Swatch and planted himself on the sofa.

"You don't know this, but every Wednesday night for the last six years, I go to CA."

"What's that?"

"Cocaine Anonymous. Before weed, I used to sell coke to support my own habit, and it took over my life. I was going through at least a gram a day, sometimes two. Every waking hour was devoted to getting it, selling it, using it, and crashing from it. I went from one hundred ninety pounds down to one hundred twenty-eight. Day after day, it chewed me up and spit me out. What's worse, I would have these fucking coke freaks busting down my door at all hours of the night to get in. That's why I switched to selling weed and why I keep everything locked in a safe."

Jasper felt like a scolded schoolboy.

"Look, I know you teach at a college and you're smart and all, but this shit is smarter than you, believe me. It'll fuck you up, it'll fuck up your girlfriend, and if someone tells you it's not physically addictive, they're lying. This shit will take you down hard."

Jasper was speechless. It was almost as if Christopher was a real friend, like a big brother.

"Didn't you say she had a kid?"

Jasper nodded.

"It'll wreck the kid, too."

"OK, OK, I get it," Jasper said. "I consider myself forewarned. She just wants a little, just this once."

In less than twenty minutes, Christopher was introducing Jasper to T-Bone. T-Bone was HIV positive and spoke so fast he was nearly indecipherable. He dressed like a hippie: lots of beads, auburn hair down to his waist, wild eyes. There was something odd about his appearance that Jasper couldn't quite put his finger on. Jasper couldn't explain it exactly, but somehow T-Bone resembled the composite sketch of a wanted felon. He peeked out through the venetian blinds covering Christopher's picture window as he went over the price points. "A hundred for a gram, one-sixty for a teener, and three hundred for an eight ball. I never mess with anything less than a gram, so don't even bother asking. It's not worth my time. And I don't front anything to anyone under any circumstances, so don't bother asking me about that either."

"Can I get some from you right now?"

"No, no, no," Christopher said adamantly. "Not here. C'mon, man, you know better than that."

So Jasper and T-Bone drove separately and met in the back row of a grocery store parking lot down the street. Jasper hustled inside, used the ATM, and returned to the cars. He learned that Bone lived a half mile away in a pink bungalow with steel-reinforced doors and bulletproof windows. There was a weapon in every room of the house, and to emphasize this fact, he pulled a pistol from beneath the driver's seat, wiggled it in the air a little, and returned it beneath his seat. "Man, I've had my door kicked in, jimmied with crowbars, the front gate to my fence blown up . . . all kinds of shit. You can't be too careful these days, but if Christopher vouches for you, that's good enough for me. Guy has the best weed in town."

Waxing all dope-poetic, T-Bone pontificated about the trick to being a successful street-level cocaine dealer.

Rule No. 1: Never get high on your own supply. (By T-Bone's own admission, he had had a history of limited success with Rule No. 1.)

Rule No. 2: Know thy clientele. No matter what, never sell to anyone you don't know. "That," he said, "is how you end up grabbing your ankles in the gray-bar hotel." Again T-Bone made it abundantly clear the only reason he was hooking up Jasper was because he trusted Christopher implicitly. In fact, he had inherited most of his customers when Christopher switched from the white to the green. Jasper was never to tell anyone, not even friends, about T-Bone.

And Rule No. 3: Never step on your product. People hook you with high-quality merchandise, and then once they have you in their clutches, start cutting it with speed or baby laxative or C&H Sugar or "God knows what."

T-Bone lived a spartan lifestyle by design so as not to attract attention, and was bound and determined not to end up in one of two yards that were common in his profession: prison yard or graveyard. He claimed to know every unmarked vehicle in the SPD fleet. One of the narcs, he alleged, drove a taxi.

They did some lines and talked for over an hour. Jasper discovered that he loved to talk (but not necessarily listen) when he was high on coke. By the time he finally made it back home, the baked chicken was cold, and Lani was asleep on the couch in her waitress uniform with Rose asleep right next to her. Jasper went in the bathroom, closed the door, and cut up a few more lines. He was dead tired but already in love with what T-Bone called "Peruvian marching powder."

Lani knocked on the door. "Hey, you in there?" She opened the door and peeked inside.

Jasper had laid out some lines on her compact mirror. He had purchased a razor blade and had chopped the little rocks into a fine, powdery dust.

"You got more?"

"No," he lied. "This is what's left of what you had."

She glared right through him. "It's not *what I had*. I had nothing to do with it. You look like shit. I think you need to get some sleep."

As she closed the door and walked away, Jasper thought, Who the fuck are you to tell me what to do in my own house? He did a couple more lines.

* * *

In the next two months, every time Jasper wanted to go to sleep, the lure of the product made him get out of bed to do more. Smoking weed was no longer enough of a counterbalance, so occasionally he did a quaalude just so he could sleep through the night. His nostrils often got so clogged from all the snorting that he had to inhale the blow through his mouth instead of his nose, a straw positioned deep into the back of his throat. He loved the way it numbed his throat, his lips . . . He loved everything about it. He could write better, teach better, think better, and he'd become adept at hiding it from Lani. He kept it in the car and never brought it inside the house. The only thing he had less of was sleep. And money. He was officially and undeniably in love with cocaine. When he did sleep, he would dream about snow, mountain climbing, and being buried in a slow-motion avalanche of cocaine.

Simple, everyday, mundane acts were exhilarating on coke, or "toot" as Jasper now called it. Cleaning the garage and scrubbing the bathtub were actually fun. In fact, his house had never been cleaner. But one Monday, after not sleeping the entire weekend, he called in sick. It was the first time he'd ever done that in three years at Emerald City Community College. By Tuesday, he reasoned, the next day, he'd sleep it off and get back to work. It was time to put the product away. The party was over. Christopher had warned him. But he didn't put it away, he couldn't put it away, the party was far from over, and Lani knew it, too, just like Jasper. She went back to sleeping in Rose's room. Practically overnight, the affection that had been rekindled between them was relegated to roommates sharing living expenses. Another by-product of life-on-blow was increased libido, and since Lani had cut him off, he went to see his therapist at Ray's at least twice a week. He was ravenously horny, and the orgasms were unparalleled on coke.

Once in English 101 class, he was lecturing about MLK's "Letter from a Birmingham Jail" when students started staring at him and pointing.

"Sir," one of them said sheepishly, "your nose."

Jasper touched his fingertips to his face. They were red with blood. "Uh, sorry, guys. Rose accidentally hit me with one of her building blocks this morning." By this time, Jasper was snorting lines between classes. Halfway through a lecture, all he could think about was retreating into the solitude of his office sanctuary and doing a line. He loved the smell of it, the rush of chopping it up, sectioning it off into lines: small, medium, and large, and the surge of adrenaline he got just before doing that first hit. Even driving to T-Bone's was a rush. The routine of it was almost as stimulating as the dope.

* * *

One Wednesday, for the third day in a row, an English 101 student visited his office, and she had a name right out of a romance novel: Scarlett Slipper. Scarlett knocked on his door, which reminded him never to indulge his vices during his scheduled office hour.

"Professor Trueblood, I'm sorry to keep bothering you, but do you have a few minutes to discuss my process essay? I hope I'm not becoming a pest. I'm still brainstorming for a topic, but I think I've finally narrowed it down to three possibilities."

"Sure, Scarlett, come on in."

"Is it OK if we shut the door?"

"Uh, sure," Jasper said. He had been advised long ago that it was best to do student conferences with the door open just so there was no appearance of impropriety, but it was not unusual for students to share intensely private matters or intimate personal anecdotes they were exploring in their essays, so Jasper capitulated and pushed the door until it clicked shut.

"I thought you settled on 'How to Watch *The Rocky Horror Picture Show.*'"

Scarlett unharnessed her backpack and laid it on the floor. She removed a spiral notebook and ballpoint pen. She was bent over at such an angle that Jasper couldn't help but look inside her vermilion-colored shoulder-padded satin blouse, at her lacy sky-blue brassiere, at her considerable cleavage. She couldn't have been more than eighteen or nineteen.

"Yeah, I decided against that. If the reader doesn't know the movie, it would be too hard to explain why people shout at the screen the way they do."

"Probably true," Jasper said. He had never experienced the film but was familiar with some of the vernacular. For instance, he knew that for never having seen it, he would be referred to as "a virgin."

"I was thinking about either 'How to Pick Your College Major,' 'How to Buy a Used Car,' or—and I'm not sure about this one—'How to Succeed in Sexual Politics.'"

Oh dear God, Jasper was thinking as he tried not to stare at her black leather pants. Pick number three! "Well, I like the first two, but they sound a little pedestrian, and the assignment is to pick an unusual topic and go beyond the obvious content. Can you tell me more about the third option?" Suddenly, he was exceedingly aware that the door was closed.

"I read a book by someone named Kate Millett called *Sexual Politics*. It was published in 1970. Have you ever read it?" She applied some cherry ChapStick and smacked her lips.

"No," Jasper said, "but in college I did read *The Feminine Mystique* by Betty Friedan. Is that close enough?"

"OK, good. Yeah, they are." She wrote something down in her notebook. "I'm not a feminist as much as I'm a human-ist, but I think Millett and Friedan make some equally valid points about female sexuality in a patriarchal society." Scarlett continued with her thesis. The semantics quickly became academic, complicated, and just as Jasper was about to tune her out, she said, "I've seen evidence of this female exploitation in my own sex life."

Jasper paused. "Really? How so?"

"Well, for example, I had sex with my sister's boyfriend." She stared at Jasper with her cantaloupe-colored eyes and then continued, "I spent the night at their apartment. We were watching movies and smoking dope when my sister crashed out. Her boyfriend made the move on me, and"—she nodded her head—"I let him. I knew it was wrong, but I did it anyway."

"And how does that relate to sexual politics?" Jasper leaned back in his chair, reminded of how much he loved his job.

"I did it because he asked me. I did it because when it comes to sex, I guess I can't say no. I did it because I lack self-esteem and because I need a guy to validate me, to make me feel attractive or worthy or . . . I don't know . . . *relevant*. It's pathetic, really. It's a character flaw I'm not particularly proud of. But I also think it's pretty sad that we live in a society where women are always supposed to be the weaker sex. We're supposed to be subservient and compliant whenever a guy gets the urge. Guys can do whatever they want and as much as they want, but a woman doing the same thing is a whore and a slut."

"Did your sister ever find out?"

She rubbed her fingers through her short red curls, crossed her legs, and took off her brown-framed glasses. "Yes. She ended up finding out from one of his friends. She forgave me. He was an asshole and she was about to break up with him anyway, so that just clinched the deal. She said that in a way I did her a favor, but she'd appreciate it if I didn't do her any more favors."

"Back to the essay. So, what's the process?"

"My process is that women should take the initiative, not feel guilty about feeling lust and having a libido, but not agree to anything they know is contrary to their gut instincts, like sleeping with your sister's boyfriend because you can't say no. Do you want to know what I hate most about it? Trying to talk to him afterward. The guy was about as smart as a pet rock. Boys my age bore the shit out of me. I know it sounds conceited, but they're so intellectually inferior. They act like wolf whistles and catcalls are going to turn a girl on. They have no idea how intoxicating the art of real conversation is. I find intellectual discourse with a man to be very stimulating. Like what we're doing right now? The ability to confidently articulate thought and emotion is a powerful aphrodisiac. It's very seductive. I like a man who knows who he is and who can articulate language eloquently, not someone like my sister's boyfriend who thinks *The Jerry Springer Show* passes for high art."

Jasper pursed his lips and nodded.

"Someone like you." She smiled coquettishly, blushed, and rolled her eyes.

Jasper felt his heartbeat quicken, aware again of the closed door. "So," Jasper said, "let me see if I follow you. The process of sexual politics is about what? Power? Control? How to get it? How to keep it?"

"It's about being willing to take control as well as being willing to concede it, depending on the situation. In a roundabout way, if you think about it, conceding control can be a form of maintaining it."

"Well, Miss Scarlett," Jasper said, "I think you just found the subject for your process essay. Consider the topic approved." To make it look official, Jasper made a check mark next to her name in his grade book. "If you don't mind my saying so, I guess I've always been sorta the opposite of your sister's ex and guys like him who are bold and aren't bashful about making the first move. Women scare me. They always have. I don't speak body language, so I don't know when they're sending me signals. If they wink, I assume they have a speck of dust in their eye. If they say something provocative, it doesn't register on my radar.

Maybe I'm too afraid of rejection. When I was younger, if I ever did manage the courage to admit I had feelings for a girl, she'd always tell me the same thing, she didn't like me *in that way*, and I would always respond with the same thing: 'OK, thank you, I'm just going to run in front of a gas truck now. Have a nice day.'"

She laughed. "Really? You were shy?"

"Oh, was I ever. I suffered from the 'best friend syndrome.' Growing up, girls were quite comfortable telling me all about their guys and their sexual escapades, like I was one of their girlfriends. They would get dressed right in front of me. I always hated that."

Scarlett wrote something else in her notebook. "Can I tell you something?"

Jasper nodded.

"Last week I told my mom that I wanted to be an exotic dancer. Strangely, she didn't seem too surprised. I was expecting her to protest, to forbid me, or at least to dissuade me, but she didn't. Not at all. She just suggested I get back on Prozac. I have a girlfriend who strips. It pays for her school, her car, her apartment . . . and it's not contrary to her instincts. She really likes it. In fact, she told me she loves it." Scarlett ran her fingers through her red curls again. "Professor Trueblood, do you think that stripping is morally wrong?"

Jasper immediately thought of Ginger Snap. "I don't, but it doesn't really matter what I think. What do you think?" And suddenly, he had an epiphany about Ginger Snap. Maybe it was that Plexiglas partition that allowed him to be genuine with Ginger Snap, to be brutally honest in a way that he wasn't with Lani or Daphne, or anyone else for that matter. It was safe.

"I don't know how to say this exactly," she said, "so I'm just going to say it. You have the dreamiest eyes I've ever seen."

Funny, Jasper was thinking the same thing about her. He really did love his job. "Thanks. You too."

She scooted her chair closer to him.

His heart began to percolate, and he wondered if she was about to do something for extra credit.

"I have to catch my bus, but I want to ask you one more question." She proceeded to unbutton her blouse in front—six cloth buttons in all—and unfasten her bra in back. Her breasts fell out; she cupped them in her hands and smiled. "Do you think these are big enough to be a stripper?"

Jasper noted there was a birthmark the size of a thumbprint just above her left nipple. He reached out and held her breasts in his hands. She placed her palms on top of his hands. He knew it was wrong, just as she had known it was wrong with her sister's boyfriend. He realized this brand of independent study could get him fired, and suddenly, his office seemed like an academic version of Ray's Pleasure Palace. But he did not stop.

Finally, she said, "I have to go catch my bus." She fastened her bra in back, buttoned her blouse in front, and retrieved her backpack. "I really like your class," she said and winked. "By the way, were you successfully able to interpret that wink?" She smiled.

On the way home, Jasper knew he had crossed some sort of line, some code of ethics. He pulled over at a nearby park, snorted a couple lines, and smoked half a joint so he wouldn't feel quite so unethical. He decided that instead of wallowing in shame, the most prudent thing to do would be to consult his intrepid therapist in Booth 12.

CHAPTER 12

HOW TO STOP STARTING

Jasper was feeling very protective of Ginger Snap these days—strangely territorial, so much so that he shot the c.o.p. exiting from her lair a derisive sneer after having to wait nearly twenty minutes for Booth 12.

She stared at him through the glass for several seconds. "Well, if it isn't my professor-slash-stripper." She smiled, then said the line Jasper longed to hear. "Tell me what you want."

Ginger turned up the music a little and started to dance. Jasper did not masturbate. She gyrated her peachy hips. Finally, Jasper picked up the phone.

Ginger responded in kind.

"I'm a terrible person."

"Why is that?"

"Because I'm doing cocaine almost every day. Because I cashed in the IRA my biological mother left me in her will—over $12,000—and I've snorted every dime of it. And the house that I inherited from her? I'm about to miss the second mortgage payment in a row."

Ginger slipped into her terry-cloth robe, sat down, and sipped from a small juice box.

"And that's not all."

Ginger squinted and twirled a blonde dreadlock.

"One of my students just took off her top in my office, and I didn't do anything to stop her. In fact, on the contrary, I gave her girls a nice firm squeeze. And truth be told, I must admit they were quite magnificent, but I could get fired for shit like that."

"You've been a bad boy, Professor. Mama is gonna have to punish you."

Jasper felt nauseous. "I have everything I ever wanted," he said. "A girlfriend, a family, a dream job . . . Why am I doing this? Why am I wrecking my life? And why do I always need to see you?"

Ginger closed her eyes, pinched her nipples, and arched her back.

With over twelve minutes left on the timer, Jasper hastily exited the booth without saying goodbye. He suddenly had a crisis of conscience and vowed he'd never return to Booth 12. He needed to go home and patch things up with his family. He did not like the person he had become, and he snorted a couple more lines in the parking lot to prove it.

* * *

The next day in English 101, when Scarlett Slipper did not make direct eye contact, Jasper was unsure whether it suggested remorse, coyness, or something in-between. In his office after class, as he was finishing the remnants of an eight ball he had purchased from T-Bone two days earlier, he realized he was on a collision course with a complete financial catastrophe.

He still owed money on his car. In addition, even though the bank took out money for the considerable taxes and penalties that Jasper would owe the IRS for the early withdrawal of the IRA, he was delinquent in property taxes to the tune of $2,280. Plus, there was the second consecutive missed mortgage payment. If I were smart, he thought, I would apply for an equity loan or a second mortgage. However, at the moment, he wasn't feeling very smart at all, in fact, quite the contrary. He was still wearing the same three dull suits to work—brown, gray, and blue pinstriped, all in desperate need of dry cleaning. His savings account was nonexistent. Lani had been paying for almost everything: groceries, utilities, and Rose's day care. Not only had she long since stopped sleeping with him, they barely spoke. And what Jasper wasn't spending on coke, weed, cocktails, or therapy at Ray's Pleasure Palace, he was spending on his newest vice—cigarettes. At least it was legal. Plus, he hadn't called his dad since returning from Guam. His relationship with the old man was always a reclamation project, a tenuous work in progress.

Late one afternoon with a dollar bill up his nose, there were three rapid knocks on the office door and it suddenly swung open. Panic-stricken and heart pulsating, Jasper pulled off a nimble act of abracadabra and managed to place a notebook on top of the lines he'd laid out on the framed glass picture of his dearly departed mothers, both adoptive and biological, juxtaposed in the same frame.

"Sorry to disturb you—" The gray-shirted custodian was holding the master key, his cart of cleaning supplies visible in the hallway. He looked down at Jasper's desk, then averted his glance. The lower half of the glass was still visible with traces of the white powder. Rather than emptying Jasper's wastebasket, he simply said, "I'll come back later."

* * *

Several days later, during final exams week, Jasper was in the back of the college parking lot, leaning across the front seat of his car and kissing Scarlett Slipper. Since their little soiree in his office, he'd been giving her rides home to her sister's apartment almost daily, and while her sister was at work, their liaisons had escalated to extracurricular activities that were well beyond academic. As it turned out, Scarlett Slipper was insatiably sexual, and when it came to sexual politics, she could run for mayor and win in a landslide. Coincidentally, she was also quite fond of cocaine. Just then, one of the school's security guards walked by and shot him the evil eye. "Shit," Jasper said. "Fucking shit!"

* * *

The next day, Dean Wright was waiting as Jasper walked out of his ESL final. "Professor Trueblood, may I see you in my office, please?"

"Of course," Jasper said. "Right now?"

"Yes, right now."

"Is there anything wrong?"

"Let's talk in my office."

Jasper followed him. A few students cleared a path as they marched up the twelve steps to the second floor of the Administration Building.

"Have a seat," the dean said.

Jasper tried to maintain a positive attitude. Maybe another tenure-track position was opening. Maybe he would be encouraged to apply again since he had gotten so close last time. But his cautious optimism came to a screeching halt when Dean Wright closed his office door with considerably more force than was necessary, bordering on a slam.

"I'm not sure if you've met Mr. Johnstone, our director of security."

"Uh, yes, sir." Jasper noticed the paintings on the far wall, and from what he remembered of his art history class, they were from the rococo period, eighteenth century, French. In stark contrast, on the adjacent wall were photographs of what Jasper assumed were Dean Wright's family members as they all wore the same black-framed glasses. "I mean, I've never met him personally, but I've seen him around. I believe he usually says a few words at convocation every year, doesn't he?" Then it hit him. The security guard in the parking lot—I am about to get fired!

"This morning, Mr. Johnstone stopped by my office. One of his men reportedly witnessed you kissing someone in the parking lot yesterday, one of your students. Do you deny this allegation, Professor?"

Fuck, fuck, fuck, he thought. "No," he said, and then his voice lowered several octaves. "No, sir."

"Good, because there are video cameras that have you on tape. Before you say anything else, Mr. Trueblood, listen carefully to what I'm about to say."

It was the first time Jasper had ever heard Dean Wright address an instructor without the title *Professor*.

"Jasper, you are well liked and respected at this institution. People have their eyes on you. Your teacher-course evaluations are some of the best I've ever seen, and I've been at this place for over twenty years. But let's be crystal clear. My late father was in the navy and had a penchant for colorful colloquialisms. One of his favorites was 'Don't shit where you eat.'"

Jasper bowed his head. He folded his hands and exhaled.

"What would happen, hypothetically let's say, if you gave this student a high grade, and it was purported that you were playing favorites? The academic equivalent of quid pro quo. Worse yet, what would happen if this student, I believe her name is Miss Slipper, received a grade she disputed and made public your private indiscretions?"

Jasper nodded. He felt as if he were facing his own father, and this was the point where his father would have removed his belt with a swoosh and instructed Jasper to assume the position. "Y-yes, sir." His voice quivered.

Dean Wright stood up. "Son, you're an adult, and legally she's an adult, and you're a human being with emotions. We all have emotions. But in this business, you must be beyond reproach. Otherwise, the college could be vulnerable to reprisals and even litigation. Don't shit where you eat." The dean peeked up at the ceiling and made the sign of the cross, which Jasper interpreted as an homage to the dean's deceased father. "Am I making myself clear?" He put his hand on Jasper's right shoulder.

Jasper nodded. "Yes, sir."

Dean Wright said, "Good. Now don't ever let this happen again."

"You have my word on it."

The dean smiled. "Excellent. Now get your ass out there and mold the minds of our future leaders, capiche?"

Jasper looked up at him, smiled slightly, and nodded. "Yes, sir." Jasper's scarlet fever had become his scarlet letter. As he walked crestfallen out to his car, there were only two things on his mind: (a) page T-Bone immediately, and (b) decapitate that fucking security guard.

* * *

He tried to stop. Day after day, week after week, he tried to stop so hard it hurt.

Every time he ran out of blow, he would avoid the phone, pretend T-Bone was dead or kidnapped by aliens, but then he would dream about cocaine, the smell of it, chopping up the lines, rubbing his gums, numbing his life. Even when he promised himself and God and his dead mothers—and Lani—that he would never touch the stuff again, over and over he'd keep paging and popping up at T-Bone's. He didn't know how to stop starting. Once he stopped, he didn't know how to stay stopped.

"Jasper," Lani said, refusing to make eye contact as she stirred the spaghetti sauce one evening (she didn't call him *Jazz* anymore). She rarely even referred to him by name. "The bank called. They're taking you to collections. And the city keeps sending these." She handed him a large red foreclosure notice she had found affixed to the front door. "Pretty soon, they're going to take the house. I'm covering half the mortgage and all the bills for Rosario and me, but I'm not going to pay your back taxes."

"This is entirely your fault!" Jasper shouted, pointing at her. "This whole fucking thing is totally your fault! You're the one who brought that shit into the house in the first place!"

Lani opened her mouth once and then a second time, but it was as if the words were being bottlenecked in her esophagus. She broke down crying. Then Rose walked in carrying Snowball. "Don't cry, Mommy." Rose consoled her mother until they were crying in tandem.

Taped to the pantry door was a picture of Rose, a photograph originally taken in the living room, which Lani had enlarged into a poster. The front door had a beveled glass transom, and early in the morning, at just the right moment when the sun was rising, the light would disperse and cast a prism on the living room floor. One day, Lani positioned Rose on the carpet, smack-dab in the array of colors. Her little head was in shadow, but from her chin to the bottom of her torso, the sunlight cast a spectacular rainbow on the canvas of her body: violet-blue-green-yellow-orange-red. It was the most glorious thing Jasper had ever seen, at least it used to be, and he realized how far he had imploded when he stared at it, then at the two girls in his life weeping inconsolably, and felt absolutely nothing, not a speck of contrition. He got in the car and drove.

Along the Battery Street Tunnel, it occurred to him that all he had to do was punch the accelerator, turn the wheel hard into the concrete retaining wall, and it would all be over. His grip tightened and he almost did it. Twice. Instead, he drove over to T-Bone's as if the vehicle were on autopilot.

* * *

It was over a month before he and Lani had a civil word with one another. Jasper kept thinking about calling Christopher, about going to a twelve-step meeting with him, but he did not. He just kept going back to T-Bone's. Once, he literally begged on his knees for a half gram since that was all the money he could scrounge. Bone was willing to make an exception but just this once.

The next time Jasper needed money, he hocked some of Lani's jewelry at a pawnshop downtown.

One night after Lani put Rose down for bed, Jasper knocked on the bedroom door.

No answer.

He knocked again and ducked his head inside. Lani was crying into a pillow. Jasper came up and put his arms around her. She pushed him away, but he held on tighter until she finally relented and cried into his shoulder.

"You took my earrings and my bracelet. I got those from my f-f-father."

"I'm sorry," he said. "None of this was your fault. You didn't even know that coke was in your pocket. I was the one who couldn't put it down. I was the one who fucked up. This is my responsibility. I'll get your jewelry back next payday. I promise. I'll go down there before school tomorrow and put it on layaway." Even as the words left his mouth, his internal voice was whispering into his internal ear, *"Sure you will, if T-Bone is dead and every other cocaine dealer in the city moves to Shanghai."*

She cried harder. He hugged her tighter. After she fell asleep, he drove out to Ray's Pleasure Palace.

"I can't stop," he told Ginger Snap. He didn't even notice what she was wearing. "Cocaine has taken control. When I'm not doing it, I'm thinking about doing it. I dream about doing it. I hate the fact that I love it so much. What's happening to me? Less than a year ago, I had it all. I thought I was in love with Lani, but I fell in love with cocaine. It fucking owns me. My brain can't turn it off. It's like a clothes dryer with a tennis shoe banging around inside."

Ginger stared at him.

"Do you think I'm a bad person?"

"No." She paused and shook her head. "No. I think you're a sick person."

"Can I ask you a question?" He desperately wanted to change the subject.

Ginger slipped on her white robe, sat back, crossed her legs.

"This question is probably against the rules, but I'll ask it anyway. A couple weeks ago, I was teaching an essay by Malcolm X and something occurred to me. I never think about being white. Do you ever think about being black?"

Ginger laughed and twirled one of her dreadlocks. She turned off the speaker switch and picked up the red phone. "I think about being black every single day."

Jasper stared at her.

"I'll do you one better, Professor. Did you know that at one time or another, most people of color have fantasized about killing a white person?"

He paused. "Wow. Have you?"

She looked upward, then turned back toward Jasper. "I'll have to plead the Fifth on that. The thing is, I can explain it for you, but I can't understand it for you."

"I just read about two white cops down in the South shooting a black kid six times in the back because he ran from them. He didn't even have a weapon. He was just scared 'cause he had a dime bag of weed. Fourteen years old."

"People talk a lot about racism in the South, but in some ways," Ginger said, "it's even worse out West. At least in Alabama or Mississippi, when they call you 'nigger,' they're waving the Confederate flag while they do it. You know who they are. Out here, the bigots act like they're your friends and then as soon as you leave the room, they're crackin' jokes about watermelon and fried chicken. I've heard it referred to as 'polite racism.' They're not only racists, they're phonies."

"I'm a white male and I'm always angry. I can't imagine what it must be like for a black female."

"It is what you make of it. Life is ten percent the shit that happens to you and ninety percent what you decide to do with it."

They stared at one another again.

Ginger said, "Listen, if you're black or brown in this country, you can let this corrosive shit eat you alive like battery acid from the inside out, or you can do somethin' about it. You can play the race card or let the race card play you. For me, success is the best revenge. I intend to make somethin' out of my life. No excuses. Failure is not an option. Plus, as an educator you might find this amusing. Some of my black friends say I'm not black enough. I mean, seriously. Look at me. My eyes aren't brown, I'm gainfully employed, I'm Republican, I have no criminal record, and my favorite band is ABBA. You can't get any whiter than ABBA!"

The timer was down to three minutes.

"Professor, you don't have to tell me what you want anymore. Mama knows what you want. You want help. Almost every girl who works here is hooked on something, and half of them are using this place to set up tricks. It's not a sign of weakness to ask for help, it's a sign of strength. You're livin' in the problem. Start livin' in the solution. You can change. The brain has an immense capacity for neuroplasticity."

"For what?"

"Neuroplasticity. The ability to create new connections in the brain's neurons. You can change your brain: sharpen your memory, improve your intellect, recalibrate the way you think. You can even rewire subconscious thought by replacing negative self-talk with positive affirmations. But you need to ask for help, Professor, or shit's gonna envelop you like a mushroom cloud."

Jasper nodded. "It's already happening. The bomb has already been dropped."

Silence.

"Have you ever been in love?" As soon as Jasper asked the question, he knew it was against the rules. He wished he could take it back as it hung in the stale air.

Ginger Snap turned away, paused, and then turned back toward him. She pursed her lips. Her lower lip quivered slightly. "I used to be married."

"Used to be?"

"Yes. He died in an accident."

"I know it's against the rules, but can I ask what happened?"

Tears leaked down her cheeks. She began to rub the gold cross necklace dangling from her neck between her thumb and index finger. "A crane fell . . ." She hesitated and then continued, ". . . at a construction site. He was a foreman. That's why I came to work here." She wiped her eyes and whispered, "I've been wanting to tell someone that for the longest time."

"I'm sorry." The timer showed sixty seconds and he was out of tokens. He held his hand up, and on the other side, she held her hand up to his. He could almost feel her body heat through the Plexiglas. He searched the pools of her eyes as if seeing beneath the surface for the first time. The timer clicked 00:00. She uncharacteristically did not blow him a kiss or wink as the shutter dropped like a trapdoor.

CHAPTER 13

DIVINE POSITIONING

One afternoon, Jasper was in his office grading final exams when he was startled by a knock on the door. It was a young woman, and he tried to place her face but couldn't. "Hi. May I help you?"

"I hope so. I'm looking for Professor Trueblood."

Jasper nodded. "That's me. What can I do for you?"

"I believe you knew my father."

"Oh." Jasper smiled. "Here, come in and make yourself comfortable." He was careful to never close the door unless he was alone, a mistake he'd never make again. "Was he a student of mine?"

The young woman unzipped her windbreaker and sat across from him with a small teal-colored tote in her lap. "No," she said. "Is your real name Junior McPherson?"

Jasper froze. Other than his father on the telephone, Jasper hadn't heard that name in years. He smiled. "How did you know that?"

"My biological father was Troy Archer. The lead singer Troy Archer of the Unknowns? I live in Kansas City. I'm in town with my stepdad. My adoptive dad. He's a lawyer and a total yuppie, probably the opposite of Troy. He's at a conference in Tacoma for the National Bar Association, and I asked if I could tag along because I wanted to meet you."

Jasper, typically not prone to speechlessness, felt like his vocal cords had been tongue-tied into a slipknot.

"Bud Black told me about you. Bud said he knew you. I guess he and Troy were best friends."

Jasper nodded, incredulous. These were names he hadn't heard in over a decade. "I used to work for Bud. He ran Troy's ranch in Tucson." Jasper sat back in his chair. "Bud was a genius. He could make clocks run backward. Bud could do anything."

Felicity was a tall, angular girl with soft doe eyes and dishwater blonde hair that bounced and cascaded well past her shoulders. "Bud said that if I wanted to know the real Troy Archer, beyond the rock star exterior, I should come see you. He said that the two of you buried Troy at sea."

Jasper laughed. "Well, we sailed his ashes down the Mississippi River on a makeshift raft. Is Bud still blind? Sometimes his sight would come and go."

"Bud is not blind," she said. "In fact, he's taken up oil painting, and he's absolutely amazing. You should see his stuff. But it's not all good news. He's got a bum ticker. Heart problems, y'know?"

"Oh," Jasper said. "Oh . . ." And for a fleeting but visceral moment, Jasper could feel Bud's presence in the room, a phantom warmth that had filtered through the xylophone of his rib cage and settled in his chest cavity. "What's your name?"

"Felicity Alessandrelli."

"How long are you in town?"

"We leave tomorrow night."

"OK," Jasper said. "Are you free for a few hours to talk? I'll tell you all about Troy Archer."

"Sure," she said.

He assisted her with her jacket. "I've been going through some challenging times recently," he said. "I feel like Bud and Troy orchestrated this bit of serendipity somehow."

* * *

They drove over to Jasper's neighborhood in Queen Anne. Jasper wanted Felicity to meet Lani, but before they did, they stopped at the IHOP.

"See that booth over there, where that family is sitting?"

Felicity nodded.

"That booth changed my life."

She definitely had Troy's eyes. They ordered coffee.

"Back in Tucson, 1980, in the men's room of this raucous rock 'n' roll club called the Blue Parrot, some drunk pulled a knife on Troy. It's totally unlike me, but for some reason I instinctively punched the guy in the face and knocked him out cold. I had no idea the person I was defending was some rock 'n' roll icon. I was certainly a fan of the Unknowns, but Troy was dressed incognito, so I had no clue it was him. Then he took me out to his ranch, and we talked all night. That's where I met Bud.

"Eventually, Troy paid for me to go back to the Midwest and see my estranged father. Bud went with me. That's when I learned I was adopted, when I was twenty-one years old. Anyway, that changed my life. Then Troy paid a private investigator to find my biological mother, Connie, who worked as a waitress right here in this restaurant. Then he paid for me to fly from Tucson out here to meet her. That changed my life even more."

Then, as if on cue, an old Beatles song clicked on the jukebox.

Let's all get up and dance to a song that was a hit before your mother was born. Though she was born a long, long time ago, your mother should know, your mother should know.

Jasper pointed. "I sat right at that table right over there and asked Connie, a complete stranger, 'Does the day May 9, 1959, mean anything to you?'"

"The day you were born?" She sipped from her cup.

He nodded. "I showed her all the documents the investigator found for me. So, we went up to her house at the top of Queen Anne Hill and had dinner. Years later, I was shocked to learn she had left me the house in her will, along with an IRA. Anyway, we talked all night until early in the morning. The next day it was all over the news. Troy had been killed in a motorcycle accident."

"He was on his way to meet me in Kansas City. I was in fifth grade."

"Wow." Jasper shook his head. "Wow. I'm sorry, Felicity. You would have liked him. Out of the blue, he gave up his celebrity and rock star status and went to work for a suicide hotline in Kansas City. He told me it was the happiest he had ever been."

"Yeah, Mom told me about that."

"As I look back on it, Troy Archer was the turning point in my life. It's amazing how just one person can have such a profound impact."

"He cheated on my mother. They were married for a while, and he cheated on her," she said.

"I'm sorry." He didn't know what else to say. Like Troy, fidelity was not one of Jasper's strong suits.

Felicity stared at her cup.

"You want a refill? Should we order some food? It's my treat."

"No. Tell me more about him. Tell me everything there is to know about the real Troy Archer."

"OK, but let's go to my house. I want you to meet Lani. She and I were backstage in Tucson for the last show he ever played. She can tell you about him from a female perspective."

As they drove, Jasper explained how Connie never let on that she was leaving the house to him, much less her IRA. He had no idea. And when he relocated to Seattle, he got a master's degree and started teaching. "Did Bud ever tell you about Thyme Market?"

She shook her head. "Nope."

"OK, you might not believe this, but I swear it's true. I was working as a cashier in Tucson at a little place called Thyme Market. One night, I accidentally left the back door unlocked and a transient snuck in. He used to hang around the neighborhood, and we called him King Rat. He was a sad case. He wore the same clothes every day and rooted around in the trash cans for food. Anyway, Troy had this propensity, this . . . *need*, to hang out with street people. Vagrants, transients, homeless vets. He would do it surreptitiously, never letting on that he was wealthy or famous. He wanted to observe them in their natural habitat, so to speak. He wanted to see what made them tick. He was fascinated and, to be honest, I think even a little obsessed with them, with their plight, with how they got the way they were. It's a long story, but it turns out that Troy was with King Rat that night. They both managed to get inside the store together. King Rat fell asleep and the cops found him the next morning. I got fired over it because I had left the back door unlocked. It wasn't until later that I met Troy in that restroom and punched that guy. When Troy and I talked that night out at his ranch, we both kinda realized we were intertwined in the middle of this bizarre coincidence.

More than saving him in that restroom, Troy felt responsible for me getting canned, even though I was the one who screwed up with the door. Eventually, I moved out to his ranch and, like I said, worked for Bud. It was the hardest job I ever had, but at least I had a nice tan and none of this." He patted his stomach.

Felicity kept asking questions and Jasper reconstructed it all, scaffolding one flashback on top of another. He was starting to feel like the old Jasper again. Felicity was the first female in months he hadn't lusted after. When they got back to Jasper's place, Lani was hospitable, and Rose asked Jasper to play with "Mr. Bosworth." Later, as Jasper gave Felicity a ride back to her hotel, he felt his life making a comeback, correcting its trajectory. That night, Jasper would look up the word *felicity* in the dictionary: "the state of being happy, especially in a high degree; bliss."

There was a poem in there somewhere.

* * *

For six weeks after his visit from Felicity—precisely forty-three consecutive days and nights—Jasper hadn't done a single line of coke, smoked dope, or had so much as one cocktail. He even stopped smoking cigarettes. He considered Miss Felicity to be exactly what he needed, exactly when he needed it—divine positioning—the impetus to catapult him back to sanity. It was a Saturday night, and Lani had to be up early for church in the morning. (Jasper had long since given up accompanying her.) Rose was asleep on the couch, and he was grading midterm exams with the TV on in the background.

"Can you carry her to bed?"

"Sure," he said.

"Good night."

"Hey."

Lani stopped midstep. She was still facing the other direction.

"Are you and I ever gonna sleep in the same bed again? You know I've been clean for almost two months now."

She paused. "Good night."

Two hours later, he was still fixating on it, obsessing over it, resenting it relentlessly. He did his worst thinking alone and late at night. He became increasingly indignant that she was still punishing him in his own house. By substitute teaching and putting in time as a tutor, in addition to his regular schedule, he had even bought back her jewelry from the pawnshop, made the delinquent mortgage payments, and created a payment plan to satisfy his property tax debt, thereby protecting the house from the foreclosure vultures circling overhead. Why can't she let up? he thought. Why can't she cut me some slack? He was paying bills on time and repairing the broken glass of his life. Why can't she give me a break? Why is she always on my ass?

After she went to sleep, he decided to page T-Bone. It would be a grand finale, just one last little gram for old times' sake. She would never have to know. He left Rose sleeping on the couch, her chest rhythmically inhaling and exhaling from one dream to the next. He tucked her fuzzy yellow blanket all around her and, remembering the plaque on the bedroom wall, gave her a kiss on the forehead.

> *Always kiss your children goodnight, even if they're already asleep.*
> —H. Jackson Brown Jr.

* * *

Despite a feeling of foreboding, of portent, of something Scarlett Slipper would consider "contrary to his best instincts," Jasper drove out to T-Bone's. He parked down the block and, upon approaching the house, unlocked the gate and let himself in, walking past the overgrowth of azalea, wisteria, bougainvillea, and the familiar warning signs adorned with crude drawings of skulls and crossbones: Beware of Dog; Trespassers Will Be Shot on Sight. He knocked on T-Bone's front door, listened to the familiar barking of the maniacal watchdog Cujo, then he waited for the clicks of the three-bolt locks. He purchased a gram and did a couple of lines at the kitchen table while Cujo stared provocatively from the other room. The vicious canine was a Rottweiler and Bernese mountain dog mix and, according to T-Bone, at a weight of 250 pounds, larger than any Seattle coke freak and with much sharper teeth. The animal was trained to stay in the adjoining room whenever T-Bone made a business transaction. The most interesting fun fact about Cujo, though, was that he was fluent in French.

"Asseyez-vous, stupide chien."

"What did that mean?" Jasper asked.

"Sit down, stupid dog."

"Oh."

T-Bone poured four shots of liquor into a glass that was once a jelly jar. "You wanna drink?"

"Uh, sure, I guess so. Hell, why not? That looks kinda strong, though. What is it?"

"Four shots of Bacardi 151. When I'm feeling a little frisky at the end of the night, I like a nice 604 to help me sleep. A 1208 if I'm feeling dangerous. Once I had an 1812, but I paid for that the next day."

T-Bone poured him four shots and they clinked glasses. "Cheers," he said. "Bottoms up."

Jasper chugged his 604. It was like drinking napalm.

A few minutes later, the phone rang and Bone answered it. He placed his free hand over the mouthpiece and whispered, "It's for you. Are you here?"

Jasper winced, hesitated, and then grabbed it. "Hello. No. No, of course she's not with me. What kind of question is that? If I were at T-Bone's, why the fuck would Rose be with me?" He placed the receiver back in the cradle with a bang.

"The high command?"

Jasper nodded. "You believe that shit? If she was able to deduce that I came over here, why would she think I'd bring Rose? She knows what I do here. It's not a secret. Why the fuck would I bring a child?"

They did some more lines, this time out of T-Bone's supply, talked about nothing for a while, and then T-Bone said, "You know, you could get a lot more bang for your buck if you freebased this shit or, better yet, mainlined it." He pulled a cookbook off the kitchen shelf that was really a stash box, opened the cover, and inside was a red velvet pouch containing a spoon, cotton balls, a green Bic lighter, rubber tourniquet, and several syringes. "You wanna try?"

Jasper considered it—not a bad way to go out for his last hurrah. "Maybe another time."

"You wanna another 604?"

"No, thanks. I gotta get goin'." He decided to head home to find out what the hell was happening and didn't even make it past the grocery store parking lot before he pulled in to do another line. He didn't have a razor blade or credit card, so he dumped some of the powder out on a cassette tape case, rolled up a dollar bill, and snorted it, rocks and all. He remembered how much he loved the taste of it as he ingested it into his nose, felt it drain down his nasal passages, and drip down the back of his throat. Bone had the best nose candy. Jasper rubbed some on his gums and inner lips. He checked the rearview; as usual, his eyes were wildly dilated. He went into the store for a pack of cigarettes and a quart of beer to counteract the demon rum. For old times' sake. One last tryst. He finally had a handle on it. It was different this time. It was completely under control. The headline of the *National Enquirer* read "Scientists Prove Adam and Eve Were Astronauts."

Halfway home, he pulled into a park-and-ride lot to do a couple more lines. He tapped some out onto the cassette case, but as he turned to look around for cops, he accidentally knocked the cassette tape off the center console and all the coke spilled on the floor. "Fuck!" He opened the car door, bent over, and with his dollar bill snorted traces of white powder off the mat along with dirt, sand, and whatever else was down there. Maybe I am an addict, he thought. But how can I be an addict? I still have a car. I still have a house. I still have . . . stuff. He finished the quart of beer and tossed the bottle in the grass.

As he sailed past Tower Records and up Queen Anne Hill, he turned onto his block, and in front of his house was an ocean of flashing lights: cop cars, news crew, ambulance. He turned off the stereo. His heart palpitations approached cardiac arrest. He reached into his shirt pocket and swallowed the rest of the coke, wrapper and all. Mrs. McCready was the first to rush up to the car. She was soaking wet yet it wasn't raining.

"Hurry, Professor Trueblood. They're about to take her away."

Jasper ran to the front door. There was Lani in her nightgown with red, tear-streaked cheeks. The ground-level window was wide open. Jasper thought it must have been a break-in. Then he saw Rose. Her eyes were closed, her hair was dripping wet, and her diminutive little face was blue. She was wrapped in a white blanket and hooked up to a respirator in the back of the ambulance. And just as Jasper asked Lani what happened, he knew.

"Mrs. McCready found her lying facedown in the koi pond," she said.

"Oh my God, oh my God, oh my God," Jasper said. "Is she alive?"

An EMT cloaked Lani in a white blanket identical to Rose's. She was assisted into the back of the ambulance and glared hauntingly at Jasper as the vehicle hit its siren and sped away.

"Is this your house, sir?" a female police officer inquired.

"Is the little girl alive?"

"The neighbor was performing CPR when the ambulance arrived. We don't know her status yet. We aren't quite sure how long she was in the water. Is this your house, sir?" the officer repeated.

"Yes."

"May I please see your identification?"

Jasper offered his wallet.

"Would you mind removing the license for me, sir?"

As Jasper tried to extract it from the plastic slip, his hands were shaking demonstrably, and a pack of orange Zig-Zag rolling papers fell out into the street.

The officer picked it up and held her flashlight up to Jasper's eyes. "Sir, have you been using any kind of narcotics this evening? There's a white powdery substance all over your nostrils."

"No, ma'am. I went out earlier for chocolate milk and a powdered doughnut." He lit a cigarette.

She squinted at him. "Your eyes are extremely dilated, sir, and you smell like alcohol. How much alcohol have you consumed tonight?"

"None."

She nodded. "OK, would you mind stepping over to the squad car with me?"

Mrs. McCready and the TV cameraman watched as he followed the officer. He stood spread-eagle with his hands placed on top of the police cruiser as instructed. The officer frisked him. "Would you mind if we search your vehicle, sir?"

"No," Jasper said, voice quivering. He remembered there were traces of blow on the floor. "But is that really necessary considering all that's happened?"

"Yes, sir. I'm afraid it is. Please have a seat in the back of our vehicle. Watch your head. I'll be right with you." She and her male partner used their flashlights to search Jasper's Honda. More cops arrived. One of them proceeded to wind yellow caution tape around the front of the house.

It's a dream, Jasper thought. It has to be a dream.

* * *

As much as he wanted to go to the hospital, Jasper complied with the officer's request to stay at home and not drive. Miraculously, he was not under arrest. The cops and reporters left. Jasper was alone. He called the ER four times and still there was no report on Rose's condition. More than anything else in the world, he wanted to go back and see T-Bone, but he had only eleven dollars left in his account until payday. He searched all his stash spots to see if any residue remained. A mirror he could lick. Remnants of a gram he had forgotten about. He accidentally stepped on one of Rose's windup toys and was startled when it started its tinny, mechanical refrain.

> *Mary had a little lamb, little lamb, little lamb.*
> *Mary had a little lamb, its fleece was white as*
> *snow. And everywhere that Mary went, Mary*
> *went, Mary went, and everywhere that Mary*
> *went, the lamb was sure to go. It followed her to*
> *school one day, school one day, school one day.*
> *It followed her to school one day, which was*
> *against the rule.*

Jasper stared at CNN and began to read the encyclopedia, starting with the letter *a*. He found his notebook and wrote down the meaning of words that struck him, of the words left in the English language with which he was still on speaking terms.

addiction: the state of being enslaved to a habit or practice or to something that is psychologically or physically habit-forming, such as narcotics, to an extent that its cessation causes severe trauma.

The next morning, still wearing his clothes from the night before, Jasper was startled awake by the phone. It was Lani. Rose was in pediatric ICU. She was in a medically induced coma and on the critical list. If she survived, brain damage was a possibility. The dream was not only real but also grisly and heinous.

"Police officers asked a lot of questions about you and me. I think we need an attorney."

"For what?"

"Child neglect, child endangerment . . . I don't know. Mrs. McCready told them that Rose had tried to crawl out of that window on several occasions." Lani instructed Jasper not to come to the hospital. They needed to maintain a healthy distance from one another.

"Why?" Jasper said. "I love you. I need you. I have to see Rose."

"Look, with Marcel, I knew I always had to walk on eggshells, but at least I knew who he was. With you, I never know what to expect. I have no clue who you are. You're the kind of person who would steal someone's wallet and then help look for it. I can't trust you. I'm tired of you making up the truth. I'm tired of being addicted to your addiction. Don't forget, I've been down this path myself, which is why I left Guam in the first place. I know what I'm talking about."

"Please, baby, don't. *Please.* I'm sorry. I am so sorry. Don't give up on us. Just one more chance. Christopher goes to Cocaine Anonymous. I'll go with him."

"You've said all this before. It's insulting. You're insulting my intelligence. I asked you to put her to bed, to carry her back to her room. The next thing I know, the neighbor's screaming and I'm dialing 911. Do you know what it feels like to look at your child's bloated face and wonder whether she's alive or dead, meanwhile your boyfriend is doing cocaine over at his dealer's house?"

"I'm sorry," Jasper said.

"I called Marcel. He's coming to get Rosario and me. As soon as she's better, I'm taking Rose back to Guam. We're going to try to be a family again."

"What do you mean, you called Marcel? Marcel's in prison."

"Not anymore. His conviction was overturned on appeal. I found out from my sister, but I didn't want to tell you. He was released last month."

"You gotta be kidding me."

"One of the jurors was found to be prejudicial because he had an axe to grind. He'd been fucked over by Marcel's father back in the day. More than likely, what really happened is that the judge found out Marcel was conspiring to have the judge's entire family blown up or something. Anyway, Marcel's out and they're not going to retry him. He's on his way to Seattle, so I suggest you lie low."

"Jesus Christ. That's not something you thought you should tell me, Lani, that your homicidal husband who once tried to kill me has been released from prison?" But it was too late. She had already hung up. There was no more Lani.

At that moment, as he listened mechanically to the distant dial tone, it occurred to Jasper that insanity wasn't doing the same thing over and over and expecting a different result. For Jasper, insanity was doing the same thing over and over that he knew would destroy him but doing it anyway.

* * *

Jasper kept dialing the hospital to check on Rose until he was advised by the medical staff to please stop calling, that someone would contact him if her condition changed. Jasper decided he was not going to wait around for the cops to show up and arrest him or, worse yet, for Marcel to stop by with a machete and a special *this is for killing my child* fruit basket. When 10:00 a.m. rolled around, he was the first c.o.p. to patronize Ray's Pleasure Palace. He noticed the big, pink neon woman near the marquee had short-circuited her winking eyelash; now it was just twitching as if the lady had a massive facial tic. He had spent four dollars on a pack of cigarettes and shoplifted two additional packs, so he had seven bucks to spend on therapy.

He slipped inside Booth 12 and slid in four tokens. The shutter ascended and the glass revealed a young white girl wearing yellow-tinted sunglasses. She had a pale complexion and perky breasts. There was a birthmark just above her left nipple. Jasper picked up the phone. "Who the fuck are you?"

"I'm Destiny. *Who the fuck are you?*"

"Where's Ginger Snap?"

"I couldn't tell ya"—she blew a pink bubble with her pink bubble gum and popped it—"but I guarantee you one thing, anything she can do? I can do better."

Jasper scanned inside the booth, on both sides of Destiny. "Where is Ginger Snap?"

The girl peered over her sunglasses and smiled. "What's wrong, Professor? I'm not good enough for you anymore?"

He violently kicked the wall beneath the glass and then suddenly stopped. Wait. What did she just say?

Destiny lurched back and covered herself, cowering inside the standard-issue Ray's Pleasure Palace white terry-cloth robe.

Holy shit, Jasper thought. He knew this girl. The red curls, the orangey eyes, the birthmark . . .

Scarlett Slipper.

Jasper shot her a vicious glare, stormed out, slammed the door behind him, and checked the wall next to the curtain. Ginger Snap's picture had been replaced by Scarlett's. He pushed his way past a creepy old pervert at the front desk purchasing a dirty movie. "What happened to Ginger Snap?" Jasper demanded of the clerk.

"She quit," said mullet man. "She don't work here no more."

"Son . . . of . . . a . . . bitch," Jasper said. "Where did she go? How can I get ahold of her? It's an emergency. Where's the owner? I want to talk to Ray."

For the first time ever, the clerk made direct eye contact. "I am Ray. I don't know where she went," he said, "and even if I did, it would be against the law for me to tell you."

"Fuck." Jasper held out his remaining tokens. "I want my money back for these."

"No refunds."

Jasper slammed his palm and the tokens down on the glass. "I want my fucking money back."

Ray squinted at Jasper, at the tokens on the countertop, then went into the register and fished out a few bills. "Here," he said. "Now get out."

Jasper lowered his tone, trying to sound calm, reasonable. "Please, Ray, if I give you my phone number, can you just have her call me? Please."

Ray reached under the counter, pulled out a black rotary dial phone, and said, "No, but I'll tell you what I will do. I'll call the police, and depending on traffic, it'll take them between four to six minutes to get here. So I'm giving you a head start. I suggest you use it." He dialed 911. "Yes, operator, this is the owner of Ray's Pleasure Palace on Old Airport Road. I have a customer who is aggressive and confrontational. He refuses to leave, and I'm afraid he's about to become violent. I need an officer to come out to the premises immediately before it's too late."

Jasper started toward the door.

"And don't come back," Ray warned, hand over the receiver.

"Don't worry, I won't." As Jasper made his way toward the car, he looked back and saw a pair of yellow sunglasses staring at him from a window on the second floor. As he drove away, he noted it was exactly four minutes later that the SPD came speeding past him in the opposite direction, sirens blaring, cherries flashing.

* * *

Jasper pulled into Christopher's, knowing that not calling first would piss him off royally. The Beamer wasn't in the ordained parking spot. He knocked on the door, hoping maybe Christopher's boyfriend was home, but there was no answer. Jasper wasn't sure why he'd gone there in the first place. Fuck Cocaine Anonymous, he thought. Fuck all those pathetic losers. I'm a college professor. I'm not like them. I have a master's degree.

Jasper drove over to T-Bone's. The nice thing about T-Bone was that he was always home. Jasper knocked on the door, and Bone's eye appeared in the peephole. Jasper heard the dog barking and the requisite clicks of the locks that protected the house from drug-crazed cokeheads. People like Jasper. T-Bone was wearing a wifebeater and white boxer shorts with red hearts. "You really need to page me first. How much you want?"

"Just one g."

"OK, have a seat." Jasper sat on a wooden stool at the kitchen table while T-Bone measured out a gram at his desk in the corner of the room. On the table was a .38 caliber revolver, a Saturday night special. Jasper had never held a gun before. He picked it up, placed the barrel flush against his right temple, and felt the cool relief of the metal against the body heat of his skull.

"Hey!" T-Bone screamed. "Hey! Give me that! What in the hell are you doing, man? Are you fucking crazy?" One by one he unloaded the bullets from each chamber.

"Don't worry, I wasn't going to shoot myself. I was just seeing how it felt."

"You scared the shit outta me, man. Pay me and get the fuck out before you give me a damn heart attack."

"Can you front it to me just this once? I get paid on Tuesday. Please? You know I'm good for it. C'mon, Bone."

"No way, man. I never front anything to anyone *ever*. I told you that the day I met you. If it don't make money, it don't make sense. No dead presidents, no product. Stick to the script, kid."

"Come on, Bone. I've spent how many thousands of dollars over here in the last year? Just a g 'til payday. You know I'm not gonna rip you off."

T-Bone went to the refrigerator and popped open a cold can of Fresca, then he walked over to the desk and waved the gram up in the air. "You see this? I'll tell you what I'll do, Trueblood. I'll make you the same deal I made for Christopher six years ago."

"What's that?" Jasper said in a decidedly mawkish tone. "You want me to suck your dick? You wanna fuck me in the ass? Tell me what you want." Jasper paused when he realized he had just plagiarized Ginger Snap.

"Shut up and listen. Listen very carefully, because if you don't, I swear to God you're going to regret it. I won't front it to you—*I'll give it to you*. How's that? Did you hear me? Free of charge, complimentary, on the house. On one condition."

Jasper stared at him impatiently. He could almost feel the cut of the razor blade chopping up the little rocks into fine lines, almost taste the product dripping down the back of his throat from his nasal passages.

"You have to promise never to page me or contact me ever again. Under any circumstances. No more product after today. Ever. You understand?"

"Why?"

"Look, when I didn't see you for a while, I thought you were done, but clearly you're not. So, if you wanna keep killin' yourself, that's your business. But I'm not gonna be your accomplice. Our relationship has gone from symbiotic to parasitic. I don't need your money that bad. You're desperate. You're dangerous. One last gram, that's it. Consider it a going-away present, because if you come back, you'll be going away for good. I'll use that pistol on you myself. It'll be payback from way back, understand? I'm serious, man. I'll let Cujo tear your ass apart." And as if on cue, the dog barked and drooled from the other room. *"Je jure que les choses deviendront laides."*

"Was that for me or the mutt?" Jasper said. "Because remember? I don't speak French."

"That was for you. What I said was 'I swear things will get ugly.'"

Jasper nodded. "OK, OK, I got it. Deal." He decided not to mention how ironic it was that the last time he was sitting in this chair, T-Bone was offering to stick a needle in his arm to maximize the proverbial bang for his buck.

T-Bone squinched his eyes and looked at him as if appraising a piece of pawnshop jewelry.

Jasper nodded. "You have my word on it." He would have agreed to anything. "I promise."

T-Bone sized Jasper up for a moment and handed over the blow.

As Jasper drove away, his gas tank nearly empty, he was thinking that getting banned from Ray's Pleasure Palace and his coke dealer's house on the same day had to be a bad omen. He knew what he should have been worried about was Rose, but what he was really worried about was Rose's father. In his ear, he could hear Rose saying over and over, "My daddy sick. My daddy real sick."

CHAPTER 14

THE DRAIN, CIRCLING

Jasper picked up a six-pack of beer and made it back to Queen Anne, salivating like Pavlov's dogs. He could not wait to do a few more lines and call the hospital to find out about Rose, but as he turned down his street, he panicked. An SPD squad car and a local TV news van with a satellite dish were in front of his house. Jasper felt like he was walking the gauntlet to the gallows. He pulled over, backed up in a neighbor's driveway, and turned around. There was nowhere else to go; he could feel himself circling down the drain. There was nowhere to go. Everything he needed for school was in the house. He drove down to the pay phone next to the IHOP. Rose's condition remained unchanged. He was told that Lani was unavailable. He kept imagining himself in the crosshairs of a high-powered rifle owned by Marcel, the kind in the movies with the silencer and telescopic sight. Somehow, his life had evolved into a not-very-good action movie.

Jasper had just enough gas to make it to school. Since it was Sunday afternoon, the parking lot was completely empty. He drove out to the far edge, near a stand of dogwood trees. It was raining, wind blowing, leaves trembling. He lowered the seat on the passenger side to the recline position and tried to sleep, but he knew it was no use as long as there was coke in his pocket. Sixteen hours later, after he had taken several walks around the perimeter of the campus in the middle of the night and the sun had begun to color the sky, colleagues gradually started to arrive. He was starving, but worse than that, his heart was thumping so hard that he thought he might actually be having a heart attack. Before his first class, Jasper walked into the front entrance of the college like it was just a normal Monday morning, as if nothing were amiss, like everything was exactly as it should be. He owned the place. He splashed cold water on his face in the men's room and, as inconspicuously as possible, retreated to his office to call the hospital.

Still no news.

As the campus populated, people seemed to have one of two reactions to seeing him: they either stared as if he were disfigured or they avoided eye contact altogether. There was no in-between and no conversation, not even so much as a "Good morning" or "How was your weekend?" However, as soon as he was out of earshot, he sensed whispering in the halls, people pointing in the cafeteria, and when he thought it might just be paranoia, one of his English 101 students in class said, "We saw you on the news, Professor Trueblood. How is your daughter?"

"She's not my daughter. She's my girlfriend's daughter. And we don't know yet." There was a hush in the classroom. Everyone was staring at him with one exception—Scarlett Slipper, a.k.a. Destiny, was in the back with her feet up on the desk, unabashedly chewing gum and applying nail polish. Jasper assigned an in-class essay, to read pages 99–105 from the text, and a handwritten one-page synopsis was due by the end of the hour. He didn't want to dismiss the class early, but he didn't have the heart to stand in front of them and pontificate sanctimoniously about some academic diatribe of which he could not have cared less. He sat at his desk and pretended to read the book along with them. Just when he was sure life could not possibly get any ghastlier, there was a face peeking through the window in the classroom door.

Margaret.

Jasper walked outside. Twenty-eight pairs of eyes, including Scarlett Slipper's, followed his every step.

"Dean Wright would like to see you immediately."

Even Margaret, the most congenial and benevolent soul ever, seemed to wear a facial expression bordering on contempt.

Jasper stepped back inside the classroom. "The synopsis is due tomorrow. Class is dismissed."

No one budged.

"Ahem." Jasper stared at them and audibly cleared his throat. "Did you hear me?" he said louder than necessary. "Class dismissed!"

When the last student vacated the room, Jasper marched over to the dean's office, hoping for the best but expecting the worst. Sitting with the dean were two unfamiliar men in suit jackets. The three of them stood up when Jasper entered the room. Strangers in dark suits, Jasper thought. This can't be good.

Dean Wright said, "Mr. Trueblood . . ."

Jasper only caught the rest of it intermittently, that they were detectives with Seattle PD. Dean Wright held out the framed, juxtaposed photos of Jasper's two mothers—Connie who gave him birth and Doris who raised him. On the glass were traces of cocaine, a razor blade, and a rolled-up dollar bill. "This was found on top of your office desk."

Jasper's head dropped. He knew there was no use in denying it.

One of the detectives said, "We're going to have to do a pat-down."

The other one stepped behind Jasper. "Sir, would you mind placing your hands on top of your head? Thank you. Now interlace your fingers and spread your legs. Wider, please. Toes pointed outward." The detective proceeded to reach behind Jasper's head and grabbed his clasped fingers with one hand while he began the search with the other. "Sir, do you have anything sharp that could poke or cut me?"

"No." Just then, Jasper remembered there was still some coke in his right front pants pocket.

He frisked Jasper from the hair to the shoulders to the shirt, and when the detective reached inside Jasper's waistband, Dean Wright turned the other way. Then the detective got to the offending pants pocket. He reached in, removed the tiny packet, and unfolded it to find a minuscule fraction of T-Bone's complimentary goodbye gram. He laid it on the conference table. "What is this?"

Why lie? Jasper thought. Time to wave the white flag. "Cocaine."

The detective concluded the search. Jasper was informed that he was being charged with possession of cocaine, a Schedule II controlled substance, as well as child endangerment in the first degree. Both felonies.

"I have convinced these gentlemen," the dean said, "to escort you off campus without handcuffs and without lights or sirens. As of today, you are no longer an employee of Emerald City Community College. Your vehicle will be towed to the city's impound lot, and your office possessions will be boxed up and kept in storage until such time that you are able to retrieve them or have them forwarded to you."

One of the detectives started reading Jasper his Miranda rights: "You have the right to remain silent. Anything you say or do can and will be used against you in a court of law. You have the right to consult an attorney. If you cannot afford an attorney . . ."

The words seemed to float and hang in the air like clouds on the horizon. Jasper saw the clouds, he heard the words, but they made no sense. It was the first time language had betrayed him so thoroughly.

"Do you understand these rights as they've been described to you, sir?"

"Yes. Is the girl still alive?" Jasper said.

The detectives glanced at one another as if to determine who had drawn the short straw. "I'm sorry," the one with the white crew cut said, "but no. She was taken off life support earlier this morning. The doctors were unable to save her. She never regained consciousness."

"Oh my God." Jasper put his face in his hands. "Jesus." He paused. No one said anything. Then, "What about her mother?"

"The mother is also being charged with child endangerment."

I could have driven off the road twice, Jasper thought. I could have used T-Bone's .38. The dean was visibly shaken. He removed his eyeglasses and wiped his eyes. Jasper wanted to console him and say, *I know, boss, don't shit where you eat.* "I'm sorry, Dean Wright." Jasper stopped apologizing when he recalled what Lani had said earlier, that his apologies were insulting. "What about my classes?"

"We'll have someone substitute. Do you have your grade book?"

"No, sir. It's at home."

"We'll figure it out. You've got bigger problems to contend with."

As the detectives led Jasper through the foyer, Margaret was at her desk drying her tears with an embroidered handkerchief. Jasper couldn't even look at her. "My next-door neighbor is Mrs. McCready," Jasper said loud enough for Margaret to hear. "She has a spare house key. My grade book is on the coffee table in the living room."

Margaret cried harder and turned away.

Jasper wanted so badly to see Lani, to hold Lani, to throw himself on a bed of white-hot coals for Lani; but even if he could magically transport himself to her, he could not imagine what he would say. He even felt sorry for Marcel, who would undoubtedly seek retribution. Jasper was probably safer in jail. Marcel's only child was dead, and he had not been there to protect her.

Rose was dead.

An eerie stillness seemed to settle over the campus as the detectives led Jasper to the parking lot. They approached a silver sedan, fortunately an unmarked car, and one said, "Sorry, sir, but we're going to have to use these now." After being handcuffed, Jasper climbed in the back seat wondering how he could go on after something like this, after doing something not even God could forgive. Even the lone crow atop the clock tower seemed to be eyeing him with malice.

* * *

King County Jail was an eleven-story steel-and-concrete skyscraper located in the heart of downtown Seattle. Jasper stared out the car window and listened to the chatter on the police radio as they drove into the underground parking facility. "What's next?"

The detective behind the wheel said, "Central Booking and Intake. They'll get you processed, and then you can use the phone if you'd like." He seemed especially congenial, as if he and Jasper might go fishing when it was all over. They arrived at the elevator, stepped inside, and as the doors closed, Jasper felt the life being squeezed out of him, much like the handcuffs were cutting off the circulation to his wrists. On the sixth floor,

Jasper was instructed to grab a seat in the waiting room, where a dozen or so men with chains around their waists and wrists were watching a TV bolted to the ceiling. Fortunately, he did not see any women and assumed they were booked elsewhere, in another part of the facility, which meant he would not accidentally run into Lani. He scanned the premises: blue walls, white doors, gray carpeting. As he stared blankly at the screen, he kept seeing Rose's swollen body swaddled in a cocoon of white blankets and Lani's livid stare as the ambulance drove away. He kept looking around for Marcel. He still could not believe Rose was dead.

* * *

An hour later, a large blonde woman shouted, "Trueblood, Jasper!" She was wearing a green uniform with sergeant's stripes on her shoulder, gold hoop earrings, and a plain black baseball cap. She led him to the counter. In the back of Intake, four officers were forcibly leading a man to a padded holding cell, dragging him by the feet as he twisted and screamed.

"I'm claustrophobic. No! I'll kill all you motherfuckers. No! No!"

"Wow," Jasper said. The man's muffled voice was still audible from inside the confines of the cell. He was beating against the metal door with tremendous fervor.

The sergeant eyed Jasper with a subtle air of sympathy. "Around here, Mr. Trueblood, you'll find that if you treat me and my deputies with respect, you can expect to receive the same in return. However, if you do not, if you make me angry and cause a disturbance, you can expect to get tossed into Isolation. You reap what you sow. Please look straight into the camera."

Click.

"Now turn to the side."

Click.

Jasper recognized this ritual from TV cop shows.

Mug shots.

Fingerprints.

"Now walk over to that green booth. Good luck to you, sir."

In the lagoon-green booth, a male deputy instructed Jasper to strip. His pants, jacket, shirt, shoes, socks, wallet, cigarette lighter, cigarettes, and Swatch were inventoried along with a half roll of breath mints and forty-two cents. Then, feeling naked, both literally and in every other conceivable way, Jasper complied one by one with the deputy's orders, which were articulated with military precision.

"Hands in the air. Open your mouth. Stick out your tongue. Run your hands through your hair. *Again!* Now take your hand and lift your ball sack and penis. Now turn around. Squat. Spread your butt cheeks. Turn to the right. Cough. *Louder, please!* Good. Now turn to the left. Cough. Spread your toes. Are you on any medication, Mr. Trueblood?"

Jasper hesitated at first but then admitted diffidently, "I'm addicted to cocaine."

"When is the last time you used?"

"This morning."

"All right, sir. Go over to that bin and get underwear, an orange jumpsuit, and in the bin next to that, a pair of plastic sandals. Afterward you will be taken to Medical. They will check your vitals and give you something for withdrawal symptoms. Have you had a chance to use the phone yet?"

"No."

"OK, you'll have that opportunity prior to Medical."

"What if I have to call long-distance? I don't have any money on me."

"You're in luck. Long distance is by collect call only. Next!"

By the time Jasper was issued a two-inch mattress and a paper-thin blanket, his eyelids were heavy from the smell of mothballs, and he had officially become Inmate 54372, a number he would never forget. KING COUNTY JAIL was stenciled on almost everything just in case he forgot where he was.

He sat in a corner of "the tank" with twenty other men of all races, shapes, and sizes. Some seemed absolutely lost, others right at home. He avoided eye contact and secretly took the inventory of each prisoner: that guy is an embezzler who got caught with his hand in the till, that one steals cars to support his gambling habit, etc. So far, he was not afraid of the other inmates, he was afraid of boredom. It gave him too much time for self-loathing.

Even though he did not yet know the bail arrangements, he made a mental list of all the people he was too ashamed to ask for help: Mrs. McCready, Dean Wright, Margaret, Christopher, T-Bone. Once upon a time, he might have called Scarlett Slipper, but she was no longer an option. Maybe a bail bondsman, but he had no liquid assets to use for collateral. He still owed money on the car and assumed it was only a matter of time before the house would be repossessed. Then he had a brilliant idea, or at least a better idea than anything he'd had so far. *Felicity Alessandrelli.* Yes! This was why God had sent her, to save his ass from falling off. She said her father was an attorney, and that he had been in town for a conference or convention or something. Hopefully, they were back in Kansas City by now. Perhaps Felicity, the least likely candidate of all, could summon the ghost of Troy Archer to excavate him from this pit he'd been digging. Another less brilliant idea, he realized, was the thought of how nice it would be to snort a couple of big, fat lines, smoke a joint, drink a few beers, and chain-smoke a pack of cigarettes.

"Operator, may I help you?"

"I hope so. I'd like to make a collect call, please."

"To what city, sir?"

"Kansas City."

"Kansas or Missouri?"

"Uh," Jasper said, "I'm not sure."

"That's all right," she said. "I'll check both. And the party you're calling?"

"The last name is Alessandrelli." He spelled it for her.

"One moment, please." And then, "I have a Jeffrey and Gretchen Alessandrelli in Kansas City, Missouri."

"Yes," Jasper said. "Yes, that's it!"

"I'm sorry, but by customer request, that number is unpublished."

Jasper paused. More bad karma. "I believe he's an attorney. Would you mind checking to see if there's a law firm with his name, by any chance?"

"One moment, please." Then, "I'm sorry, sir, but I'm not finding anything with that name."

"OK." Jasper exhaled. "Thanks anyway."

He realized he did not have any real friends, at least not the kind who would bail him out of jail. He was relegated to calling the person he least wanted to call. It was his only hope and would require surrendering what little remained of his dignity. The operator made the connection.

"Collect call from Junior McPherson. Will you accept the charges?"

"Who is this?"

"Sir, this is your AT&T operator. You have a collect call from a Junior McPherson. Will you accept the charges?"

"Junior? McPherson? My son? Yes. Yes, I'll accept the charges."

"Thank you, sir. Have a good evening."

Click.

"Junior, is that you?"

"Yeah, Dad, it's me."

"Why are you calling me collect? Are you all right? What's wrong, Junior? Is there anything wrong? Who is this?"

Jasper scanned the premises, at the other inmates in jumpsuits using the other pay phones, at the correctional officer
standing nearby. "Dad, I'm in a lot of trouble. I need your help."
He explained his dire circumstances as best he could. The CO
said he had two more minutes.

"I don't have much money," his father said, "but I'll help
you as best I can. I had to sell the house. I live in a nursing
home. There's a full-time nurse on each floor. Father Ross said
I needed a full-time nurse. I have heart problems and hearing problems and Alzheimer's. Sometimes I forget things.
Sometimes I forget to turn off the stove. I've been trying to call
you. Sometimes they take us to a museum. It's not that bad.
This place has an indoor swimming pool. I miss you, Junior."

"I miss you, too, Dad."

"Tell me again why you called."

Jasper tried to explain it as best he could and promised to
call back when he saw the judge in a day or two. "Bye, Dad." It
sounded like there was a faint and indecipherable muttering
on the other end, and then there was no sound at all.

"Time's up, Mr. Trueblood. Let's stop by Medical."

* * *

After Medical, as the CO led him to his cinder block cell with
cobwebs and cracked white paint, Jasper felt aches, pains, and
sadness all over his body as if he had just lost a demolition
derby. He was hoping for a pen and paper, but there was only
a well-worn copy of the Bible. He read it until falling asleep on
the bottom bunk. In his dreams, he continually heard doors
locking. In his dreams, Rose was drowning in the ocean and
Jasper was swimming as fast as he could to reach her, but the
riptide tugged her farther and farther out to sea. In his dreams,
he was always chopping up lines of cocaine.

A deputy announced, "Chow time, gentlemen! Single file! You got twenty minutes to eat!"

Jasper was led with the other prisoners in single file down to the mess hall. He was not entirely sure what time it was or even what day it was. There were no clocks. He was absolutely starving until he saw what was on the menu: an eight-ounce cup of cherry Kool-Aid, four pieces of white bread, fake watery mashed potatoes, fake peas with pockmarks, reconstituted corn, and some kind of mystery meat generously referred to as "Salisbury steak." His father would have recognized this from WWII as "shit on a shingle." Jasper hated that he had to call the old man. He hated more that he only called to save his own ass rather than show any kind of genuine concern for his father's welfare.

He donated the mystery meat to the craziest inmate at his table, who kept saying, "Do you have a shiny quarter? Do you have a shiny quarter?" The inmate then proceeded to tear open a small packet of salt and sprinkle it on the meat and potatoes. Every ounce of Jasper's muscle memory told him to rip open a new packet of salt for himself and snort a few lines.

As he tried not to stare at the guards or the other inmates, Jasper ruminated about what the nurse in Medical had said about detoxing from cocaine while taking his vital signs. First, she had asked, "Are you having any suicidal ideations? Any detailed thoughts of suicide?"

Jasper resisted the temptation to ask for a working definition of the word *detailed*. "No."

She proceeded to describe the withdrawal symptoms, which included but were not limited to anxiety, apathy, depression, dysphoria, irritability, listlessness, and paranoia. Jasper was informed that *dysphoria* was "a general dissatisfaction with life." As soon as the nurse said it, Jasper knew it would end up in the same poem next to *addiction* and *enslaved*; he just needed a pencil and paper. Other symptoms included agitation, increased appetite, and unpleasant dreams. This food was the perfect antidote to "increased appetite," but there was no respite for "unpleasant dreams." For his symptoms of detox/withdrawal, he was given two extra-strength Tylenol, a cup of water, and a "Good luck, sir."

* * *

At 11:00 p.m. nightly, the guard called, "Lights out," which was not entirely accurate. What it really meant was "Lights dimmed," and in time Jasper would learn to sleep with a towel over his eyes. At 6:00 a.m. daily, Jasper woke up to all the lights flicking on and off and a guard shouting, "Inmates, strip the bed, bring the laundry outside, and join the single-file line." Breakfast consisted of generic Cheerios; three pieces of whole wheat bread; a cold, brown, flat, circular object roughly the size of a hockey puck that was purportedly breakfast sausage; milk, and Tang. He donated the protein patty to the same bug-eyed character with the affinity for shiny quarters.

When Jasper had the chance to make another phone call, he decided to call his answering machine, knowing it would limit his message to two minutes. He was led to the vestibule where there were four phones. An inmate on his left with no teeth asked Jasper if he had any "spare crack." Jasper shook his head. "Sorry, I'm all out." The individual on his right was speaking loudly, apparently calling everyone he knew to put money on his commissary book. Jasper could not hear very well, but that wasn't really a problem. Jasper was not expecting anyone to answer his phone.

"Please leave a message at the sound of the beep. BEEP."

"Lani, I don't know where you are or if you'll ever get this message, but I'm sending it anyway. You probably know by now that I'm in King County Jail. I was informed that you had been arrested, too. The detectives told me about Rose, that she . . .

that . . . she didn't make it. I should have never left the house that night. I should have welded that window shut. It's my fault, and I know you said my apologies were insulting, but I . . . I don't know what else to say. If I could trade my life for hers, I would do it in a heartbeat. I wish I could see you." He paused. "I really do love you. Please tell Marcel I'm sorry. If I could turn back the clock and—"

BEEP.

For the next twenty-one hours and twenty-seven minutes, Jasper waited to be seen by a King County District Court judge. He was advised that sometime before the hearing, a public defender would meet with him to discuss his case. In the meantime, each minute felt like an hour; each hour felt like a lifetime. He knew nothing would ever be the same. With an innocent little girl deceased, he needed to be punished. But was any sentence punitive enough to compensate for what ended up being a crime on the eleven o'clock news and decimating the one woman, the only woman, he had ever truly loved?

Jasper now resided on Planet Shame, which was not going to be easy. Guilt is saying *I did a bad thing.* Shame is saying *I am a bad thing.* The surface of the earth was guilt, the core of the earth was shame, and now he was living smack-dab in the middle. He'd give anything to go back, to take back that one night, to take back that one decision to go when he should have stayed. All he could do now was read the Bible. Occasionally, he would fall upon a verse that provided a modicum of hope.

> Acts 3:19—*Repent, then, and turn to God. So that your sins may be wiped out. That times of refreshing may come from the Lord . . .*

Still, at the end of every passage, the brief repose was followed by the profound desire to snort a gram of blow and then point Bone's .38 at his head and finish the job by splattering the wallpaper like a Jackson Pollock painting. He supposed this would qualify as what the nurse in Medical meant by "detailed thoughts of suicide." Even Marcel would not be able to put Jasper out of his misery now, unless he could find someone in King County Jail to do the job for him. And the drab decor of King County Jail, a.k.a. King County Bed-and-Breakfast, did nothing to dissipate Jasper's melancholy. The claustrophobia, however, was not nearly as daunting as the fact that someone else controlled his entire life. A guard told Jasper he was fortunate inasmuch as at least his side of the facility had windows—eight-by-eight-inch slats—with a panoramic view of street traffic down on Fifth Avenue, where the drivers had no idea how fortunate they were to be immersed in the grinding tedium of the rat race. Additionally, day and night, there was intermittent howling, shouting, chanting, and wailing, sometimes in foreign languages. Toilets flushed. Guards on shift-change laughed. Graffiti was etched on the wall next to Jasper's bed: *Fuck KCJ and fuck you, too!* A metal sign outside Jasper's cell read in big block letters: NO WARNING SHOTS IN THIS FACILITY.

CHAPTER 15

THE GIFT OF COMPLETE AND UTTER DESPAIR

A large black man with long Jheri curls like Michael Jackson's was led into Jasper's cell. A self-locking mechanism clicked behind him, and the correctional officer walked away. That sound, the heavy percussion of metal on metal, was a constant auditory reminder of Rose, of why Jasper's freedom had been revoked. He thought of the Kris Kristofferson lyric: "Freedom's just another word for nothin' left to lose."

"Yo, G, I don't wanna get all ghetto on yo' ass since we jus' met an' all, but I'mma need you to move up to that top bunk."

Jasper's new cellmate was at least six feet two and must have weighed in excess of three hundred pounds. Jasper wasn't sure if this was when he was supposed to stand up and fight, even if he got his ass beat, just to prove himself so later on he wasn't raped or extorted out of commissary money, but he didn't have the energy to fight. The pugilist in him, what little there was to begin with, was still floating facedown with Rose in the koi pond. He rolled up his mattress, snatched his blanket, and tossed them up to the penthouse.

"Yo, thanks, G. I 'preciate it. The last time I was in here three years ago, you could still smoke cigarettes. Now they ain't no smoking. What the fuck? You believe that shit? What you go by?"

"Jasper." He shook his cellie's large, soft hand. He noticed a tattoo on his forearm: BLACK BY POPULAR DEMAND.

"My name is Delphi, but they call me Del. What you in for?"

Jasper had been told in the mess hall that *chomos* (child molesters) and Five-Os (former cops) were at the bottom of the pecking order. Delphi did not seem like either. "Cocaine," he said. He didn't mention Rose.

"There's no glory in the drug story."

"Yeah, now you tell me. Where were you when I needed you? What're you in for?"

Del shrugged his shoulders. "They say I got anger issues."

"I'm new to this," Jasper said. "I don't know how any of it works, so if I say something out of line, please don't take offense. I just wanna live through this."

Delphi made his bed and smoothed out the blanket. "I been in here six times an' I know all about three hots and a cot. They call me a 'frequent flyer.' Every time I leave this place, I swear I'll never come back, but here I be. OK, G, you want me to tell you how this shit works?"

"Yes. Please."

"Here's Del's survival guide for life on the inside. The best way to stay safe is to shank someone of another race as soon as possible. Kill 'em if you can." He reached under the mattress and ripped a piece of metal from the box spring. "Like this." He jabbed it in Jasper's direction and smiled. "Then you have the Aryan Nations to protect your ass. Maybe get a nice skinhead to give you a prison tattoo of a swastika on your arm or, better yet, the face of Adolf Hitler."

"I'm not doin' that."

"OK, seriously. C'mere." He led Jasper over to the bright silver commode. "Rule number one. You see this? This is sacred. This is our throne, our oasis in the desert." He bent down to the floor and looked up inside the rim of the seat. "When you do your business in here, after you done, you gotta clean this bitch an' make it pris-tine, yo, 'cause I wash my drawers in here. If you gonna fart or shit, tell me in advance, 'cause I don't like to hear it an' I sure as hell don't like to smell it. When you use the sink, dry it out with a towel immediately afterward. If you gonna masturbate, wait to do it in the shower. Put a garbage can in front of you and everyone'll leave you alone. I don't wanna hear no bedsprings squeakin' at night. And if you see two bruthas goin' at it in the shower, look the other way. Most of 'em are just gay for the stay. Don't get involved. Stay out of it. You know what I'm sayin'?"

"Yes, sir."

"Rule number two. Don't call me 'sir.' People gonna think you my bitch in here, an' I like pussy, not dick."

"Sorry."

"And stop sayin' you're sorry. You really is new to this shit, huh?"

"Put it this way, Del, when I woke up Monday morning, I was still a college professor tryin' to get on tenure track. I sure as hell never thought I'd end up here."

For the first time, Del looked him in the eye, then they both retreated to their respective bunks and lay down.

"Keep you a brown paper sack from lunchtime. Then keep all yo' valuables in it and hide the sack under yo' pillow at night. If someone tries to jack it, you'll hear them crinkle the paper."

"OK," Jasper said from his perch above.

"An' you ain't crazy, right?" Del asked.

"Well, probably no more so than the rest of these people."

"Good, 'cause I seen it all in here. The last time I was here, I seen one dude who they called a 'feces eater.' This dude ate his own shit 'cause he wanted outta g-pop and into ad-seg. He literally ate his own shit. You talk about a shit-eatin' grin." Del laughed. "But hey, it worked. He got his wish. If what you want is being alone twenty-three hours a day in a seventy-square-foot cell with no windows, then good on you."

"Jesus," Jasper said. "What's g-pop and ad-seg?"

"G-pop is general population. That's where we are right now. Ad-seg is administrative segregation, otherwise known as solitary confinement. Like I said, one person per cell, confined twenty-three hours a day. That's for the crazies and the troublemakers and the inmates who are considered at risk, usually 'cause of some gang shit. I remember this one crazy Mexican in ad-seg who kept scratchin' his arms so bad that he nearly bled to death. And then there was this other crazy dude who was trippin', too. He tried to pluck out his own motherfucking eyeball. So, I don't need no mo' crazy.

"And don't plug up the Poseidon, uh, the commode, 'cause all that'll do is flood the entire tier and make everything smell like a sewer. Then they'll stick the whole pod in lockdown, and everybody'll wanna piece a yo' ass. Don't steal nothing, don't be a snitch, and don't call no one a 'bitch.' Those are good ways to get yo' ass shanked. One time I was in this place, there was a fuckin' riot. It was up on the eleventh floor where the real fucksticks live. We was all on lockdown for three days. In lockdown, you can feel your sanity start to fade away. It's a lot like ad-seg. Where you teach at?"

"Past tense. They fired me. Emerald City Community College."

"Yeah, no shit, huh? Emerald City. What you teach?"

"English."

"You a long-ass way from school, my brutha. My li'l sista, Marquita, used to go to that school. She loved it. She absolutely loved that place. She used to talk about it every day after class. That's where she learned to be a chef. I wish I woulda enrolled there myself like she told me to. I wouldn't be back in this shithole again."

Jasper was not sure about the prison protocol, about how far he could take the Q and A. He had never shared a room with another guy before, except for once at summer camp. He did remember a black girl in his English 101 class named Marquita. In fact, he remembered her quite well. She wore the same jean jacket every day and red Converse tennis shoes. Her essays were good. One was about her big brother. "What kind of anger issues?"

"Listen, G, let me give y'all some free advice. It's cool wit' me, you can ask me any ole damn thing, but don't ask nobody why they in here. You'll find out soon enough. And if they ask you, don't lie. Your word is all you got in here. All these folks are waitin' to go on trial. This shit jus' a holdin' pen. It's like a storage locker. You might be in here a week, a month, a year. I know a brutha who was locked up in here for seventeen months. You got killers, rapists, bank robbers . . . ever' goddamn thing. Most of the real gangstas up on eleven, but you name it, KCJ got it. State prison is a piece a cake compared to this muthafucka.

"And if you got money, you can get anything you want in this place. *Any damn thing.* I know you got a hankerin' for that white powder jus' like my boy the DC mayor, Mr. Marion Barry, but you can also get weed, crack, smack, pills, stamps, Hostess-fucking-CupCakes . . . Anything you want. As long as you got this." Delphi reached his arm out from the bed, and Jasper looked down. Del rubbed his fingertips together.

"How do they get the drugs in here?"

"Sometimes they keister it—shove the little bags up their ass—and sometimes they swallow it, then throw it up. Usually the 'court pulls' bring it back inside. They's a few COs who sell it, too. The dope in here sells for five times what it goes for on the outside. Those dirty cops are gettin' top dollar. Then you got the pod boss, also known as the HBIC—head bitch in charge. He calls all the shots. The flow of pert-near everything bottlenecks through him. You got any money, boss?"

"Nah, I spent everything on the white powder."

"That's prolly good. The bangers got all da dope, an' once they into you, they stay into you. Some of 'em make they cellies put money on they books ever' month. They call it 'chargin' rent.' Some of 'em make their cellies wash their drawers and clean the cell. So, here's my story, G. And keep this to yourself.

"First off, I ain't no banger, I'm a welder. I got a trade and I'm damn good at it. I've welded bicycles, cars, trucks, trains, and hulls of battleships under water. You name it, I've put a torch to it. What I'm sayin' is, I'm a working man.

"Second, some hood rat raped my l'il sista. Fuckin' nigga drugged 'er at some party, and then he be braggin' to his homeys 'bout how he did this bitch. I holed up one night and caught him comin' outta 7-Eleven with a six-pack and a smile on his face. I beat his ass with a pipe wrench, threw him in the trunka my car, and let him sit there for two days. I pissed on him and then I doused the muthafucka with gasoline and threatened to set his ass on fire. He wasn't braggin' then, was he? Nah, he be cryin' for his mommy. Tell me about the bitch you did now, muthafucka. Who da bitch now?

"The judge charged me with five felonies. They gonna prolly send me to Walla Walla for an extended stay. I'm gonna catch at least a dime, maybe mo'. Judge said I shouldn't be usin' no vigilante justice. I told him I was usin' hood justice, and if it was his sister, I'da done the same thing. He kinda smiled at that. Lookin' back on it, the only thing I'd do different was light that nigga's ass on fire with a fuckin' blowtorch when I had the chance, 'cause now I in here and he out there prolly doin' the same damn thing to someone else's sister."

Jasper looked down from his bunk. "Your sister OK?"

"Nah, bro. She's a long way from bein' OK. She might never be OK again. She had to quit her job at the restaurant. She loved that job. She went to your school for culinary arts and graduated at the top of her class. She won an award and everything. Now she in a mental hospital."

"I'm sorry, Del."

"Another thing, homes, apologizin' around here? That's actually a good thing. Maybe not to me all the time, but that's smart. 'Please,' 'thank you,' and 'excuse me' go a long way, too. Just do your time. Mind your own damn business, dis no one, and respect everyone. After a while, you'll develop senses you never knew you had. Around here, you can smell tension in the air like hot buttered popcorn."

"Got it."

"You listen to rap music?"

"Not too much," Jasper said. "I'm more rock 'n' roll. You?"

"Yeah, bro. Snoop, Tupac, NWA . . . all that shit. There's no music allowed in here, so I might have to start bustin' out some of my own rhymes. You down with that?"

"Whatever floats your boat."

"Funny you should say that. That's what black people did in the belly of them slave ships back in the day. Sing. Make music with whatever you got. You know the song 'Amazing Grace,' right?"

"Of course. *Amazing grace, how sweet the sound, that saved a wretch like me.*"

"That's the one. You know where that song came from?"

Jasper shook his head.

"This British cat named John Newton. He was the captain of slave ships back in the 1700s. At night, he would hear these rhythms and beats coming from the slaves on the deck below.

It haunted him. Day and night, it haunted him. And then, voilà! He found the good Lord and wrote the tune."

"And now it's sung with bagpipes at every funeral."

"For real. By the way, do you snore?"

"Not that I know of," Jasper said. "But if I do, please don't set me on fire."

Del laughed. "You a'right, bro. Look, I saw you over there starin' out the window. The less time you spend thinkin' about what you're missin' out there, the better off you'll be in here. Instead, just focus on keepin' busy. You're a teacher, right? So, volunteer in the library. Be a tutor. Do a thousand push-ups a day. If this is your first time in, you wanna leave here better, not bitter. Whatcha lookin' at?"

"What do you mean?"

"I mean with your charge. What kinda time you lookin' at?"

"I don't even know. They told me I'd see a public defender and a judge, but that hasn't happened yet."

"OK, then get some sleep. Tomorrow I'll show you which COs are thug-huggers and which ones think they're Rambo."

Jasper listened to Delphi snore and then finally drifted off himself, his sleep punctuated by more drug dreams and nightmares about Rose, Lani, and Marcel. In one dream, he had a long conversation with Lani, who slapped him in the face while Rose was bobbing facedown in the koi pond, and Marcel was cleaning his knife. In another dream, Rose was swimming with a school of fish. Jasper woke up, sat upright in his bunk listening to the heavy breathing of Delphi below him, and for the first time in memory, resorted to something radical. He climbed down from his bunk as quietly as he could, knelt on the hard concrete, and folded his hands in supplication.

Dear God, I don't know if You're out there. I don't know if You really exist. But if You do, please send me a sign. I suspect You get quite a few prayers from this address, from people who may or may not deserve Your . . . intercession. But I could really use a miracle right about now if You happen to have one handy, a spare, maybe one You're not using, that's if You have time for another jailhouse conversion.

Then, for some unknown reason, Jasper thought of an old Moody Blues song, which he would sing to himself repeatedly in the coming days and weeks. He sang it softly with perfect pitch although he couldn't remember all the words.

But in the gray of the morning, my mind becomes confused between the dead and the sleeping and the road that I must choose.

* * *

Breakfast the next day consisted of powdered eggs, three pieces of white toast, industrial-strength glop posing as oatmeal, a carton of chocolate milk, and a cup of Tang.

"Hey, white boy, gimme your bread," said a black man with a thick scar over his right eye.

Del jumped in. "He ain't givin' you shit, Scarface. Eat your own fucking bread before I come over there and shove it up yo' black ass."

"Well, well, well, look at Del's new bitch. I always knew you was an Oreo, Del. You a white man trapped in a black man's body, huh? That gotta be hard for you. I notice you like them white cellies. They so pretty an' all. That one is a baby murderer. I hope you know that. He killed a baby."

"You better shut the fuck up, Scar, before I stick this fork down your throat."

"Fuckin' Oreo muthafucka."

"Hey, Scarface, you Al Capone–lookin' muthafucka." Del said this loud enough for the entire mess hall to hear. "I heard that when they was cuttin' you up and the surgeon left that nasty-ass scar, they removed a piece of your brain about the size of a walnut. So, I was just wondering, bro . . ." Del was in performance mode, big reptile smile, working the wire without a net. A CO would be walking in any second. ". . . is it true what they say? I'd rather have a bottle in front of me than a frontal lobotomy?"

Everyone at the table laughed except Scarface. And Jasper.

Scarface stared at Jasper. "You jus' watch. I'm gonna make that cracker my bitch."

A CO stepped up and everyone went back to silently eating.

After mess hall, Jasper was reading the Bible in his cell. "Trueblood!" the CO bellowed. Jasper assumed this was it, finally—*showtime*. A public defender would meet with him, explain the charges, and wax poetically about a plea deal. As a felon, Jasper wondered if he'd ever be able to teach again. He also thought nonstop about how Lani must hate him, how Marcel must want to dismantle him, and how expeditiously everything had gone so wrong. Cocaine was a tidal wave. He followed the CO to a room that consisted of several cubicles, bulletproof glass separating the inside from the outside.

"Trueblood, you have a visitor," the CO said.

Jasper sat down and waited, expecting a public defender. After several minutes, an African American woman took a seat on the other side of the glass. At first, in her corporate attire and without makeup, he didn't recognize her. Then, when he did, when he noticed the blonde dreads pinned up in back, he got chills and began to hyperventilate. Was it really her? Had she brought Booth 12 to him? Tears streaked his cheeks. He tried to stop crying but could not.

Ginger Snap.

They stared at one another and in unison picked up their red phones.

"You are literally the last person on Planet Earth I ever expected to walk through that door. My heart is racing."

"Ray said you came in looking for me."

"I did," Jasper said. Even though the connection was weak and static riddled, it was both wondrous and surreal to be looking at her on the other side of the glass, this time without c.o.p.'s slithering around. Unlike her typical working attire, she was dressed professionally in a black pantsuit and a crisp white shirt.

"Why were you looking for me? There are plenty of other girls to party with."

Suddenly, Jasper was the one conscious of his wardrobe, of his orange jumpsuit, of being on public display. "I needed to talk. You're my therapist, Ginger."

"Well now, instead of talking, this time you need to listen, Professor. Always assume they're monitoring every conversation you have. Also, God gave you two ears and one mouth. There's a reason for that. This is a moment when you need to listen twice as much as talk. Do you understand?"

Jasper nodded. "Yes."

"First off, there is no more Ginger Snap. Ginger Snap is permanently retired. Ginger Snap is permanently dead. So, don't ever call me that again. My name is Angela Brown. When I was a kid, my friends used to call me Angel, but I prefer Angela. I have no middle name, I'm twenty-nine years old, and I'm from Nashville, Tennessee. I have a ten-year-old daughter named Samantha." She pressed a snapshot of the little girl against the glass. "Last year I finished my poli-sci degree from the University of Washington, this year I start law school at Seattle U. You with me so far?"

Jasper also had no middle name. He nodded again.

"I told you about my husband. You remember that?"

"Yes. He died in a construction accident."

"That's right. Two and a half years ago, a crane collapsed on the jobsite and broke his neck. I didn't know it at the time, but he was up to his eyeballs in debt. There was an out-of-court settlement with the construction company after he died, but it was barely enough to cover the funeral expenses, much less his bills. I worked at Ray's to pay off what he owed, then I worked at Ray's to support my daughter and me, so I wouldn't have to take out loans for law school. And before you ask me why I came here today, I'll tell you. First off, Ginger Snap, God bless her, never had a customer quite like you. You were different. You treated me . . ."—her voice trailed off momentarily—". . . with dignity and respect, like a real person. I appreciated that, more than you know. I needed that. The second reason I came here is because I was sitting at home last Friday night, watching the eleven o'clock news, innocently minding my own business, and there you were. And I remember very distinctly thinking to myself, I've never seen another human being who looked so in despair. So alone. That's why I came here today."

Jasper wiped his eyes.

"I'm a golf fan with a seven handicap. I'm an Aquarius, past president of the PTA, and I collect ceramics. I read voraciously, everything from the *Wall Street Journal* to erotica and romance novels. I think I can help you, but I have one question first, and you have to promise to answer truthfully."

Jasper almost called her Ginger. "OK, Angela. I promise."

"Were you being honest when you said you were a college teacher? I really need to know that."

"Yes. Emerald City Community College. I told you that."

"I know, so I called them to check, but all they would tell me was the date of your departure and that you were not a candidate for rehire. They wouldn't confirm whether you were actually an instructor."

"I was. I taught English. My cellie's sister was in one of my classes."

"You swear you're being a hundred percent honest?"

"Look, you can believe this or not, but as far as being honest, you're the only person I've been completely honest with in a long damn time."

Angela sat momentarily motionless, then, "I believe you mean that. I really do. If you're willing to be honest, maybe I can help you. Here's what I know about your case. Some of this is what you told Ginger Snap at Ray's, and some of it I found out on my own." She twisted one of her dreads the way she used to in Booth 12.

"Your name used to be Junior McPherson, no middle name." She smiled a little. "You are adopted, an only child, and from the Midwest. Your adoptive mother died of cancer when you were nineteen, and you subsequently became estranged from your father. You moved to Tucson, Arizona, changed your name to Jasper Trueblood, and for a while attended the university. How am I doing so far?"

He nodded.

"You broke up with someone named Daphne because she was unfaithful to you, so you decided to seek out the former love of your life, a woman from Guam named Lani. She eventually moved in with you along with her daughter. Late one night while you were out and the mother was asleep, the little girl slipped out of a ground-floor window and drowned in a fishpond. Is that accurate? And again, you should assume that they're listening to everything we say, so don't lie, but don't say more than you mean to."

Jasper could feel the tears coming again. "Yes."

"Here's what else I know, and you'll just have to trust me on this. Did you ever wonder how the TV news people got to your house so fast that night? I'll tell you how. Because one of the EMTs is dating a producer at the TV station who just so happens to be my best friend. Her EMT boyfriend fed her the information. She gave me the name of someone to contact at the DA's office whose identity I can't reveal. This individual in the DA's office told me in strict confidence that these charges are politically motivated, that the whole thing is a trumped-up ploy to gain some political traction for the DA, who's running for reelection. We're in an election cycle. You're a pawn in their reelection campaign." She glanced up toward the ceiling. "And if they hear that—*good!*" She held her middle finger up to the camera.

"What happened to the girl is a tragedy, Professor. A bona fide tragedy. No one is disputing that. But it was an accident. The mother is going to be allowed to leave Washington because it was determined she's a political liability. They're going to let her take the girl's body back to Guam for a funeral. None of this has happened yet, but I was assured it would all go down in the next twenty-four hours. I mean, how would it look if they went after the mother of a dead girl who accidentally drowned? Make no mistake about it, the accident happened on the mother's watch, not yours. If anyone was to be charged, it was her."

"I was supposed to be there."

"When you left the house, the mother and the girl were asleep. You ran an errand and came back to this horrific nightmare. It was an accident. Catastrophic? Yes. Cataclysmic? Yes. But it was an accident. The endangerment charge is bullshit, especially a felony charge, and a good attorney will get it dropped. As for the narcotics rap, for the minimal quantity you had, you plead guilty, go to drug court, and get into a treatment facility. After that, you'll have a year of piss tests, and if you don't do something stupid beyond belief, your record will be expunged. At some point, you'll even be able to teach again."

The CO stepped in. "Five minutes."

"This," Jasper said, "is when you put in the rest of your tokens."

Angela smiled and laughed a little. "I'm glad you haven't lost your sense of humor, because you're gonna need it. I am here to tell you there is reason for hope, Jasper Trueblood. There's a Persian poet from the thirteenth century named Rūmī. Ever heard of him?"

Jasper nodded. "Yes."

"Rūmī says, 'The wound is the place where the Light enters you.' That's one of my all-time favorite quotes. I guess you could say I got a thing for good quotes. Anyway, I'll be back next week. In the meantime, let the Light enter you. Lean toward the Light. Your public defender will advise you to plead 'not guilty.' You'll be seeing the judge today, too. I've been told the bail will be abnormally high, and no matter how much the PD objects, they will not let you out on personal recognizance. Again, politics. Down the road, you'll get another public defender, the one who will represent you. It could be weeks, it could be months, but hopefully by then I'll already have a real attorney lined up. I have someone in mind. He won't be cheap, but you can arrange to make payments over time. He's a good man and a trusted friend. He helped me when my husband died."

"Why are you really doing this for me? I mean, I know you saw me on TV and all, but beyond that."

She stopped playing with her hair and security badge. "If they aren't charging the mother, they can't charge you. Again, it's politically motivated. Like I said, you're nothing but a pawn in a real-life chess match. Also, I would never tell what I'm about to say to you, or anyone else when I was at Ray's, but when I was five days old, my biological mother left me in a phone booth in downtown Nashville. They have a name for people like me: *a foundling*. A mailman took me to a hospital, and to this day, I have never stepped foot in a phone booth. Foster care was pretty rough. I got hardwired to trust no one. My heart adjusted to the darkness at a young age. I became calloused. I refused to let the Light in.

"And then a teacher saved me. Someone like you. I went to parochial school, and one day at recess, a boy threw a rock. It skipped off a toolshed and hit me in the mouth. It knocked out my front teeth, and for months, the nuns would let kids call me names like 'the cave' and 'choppers.' Then in fifth grade, I had a lay teacher, a white woman named Mrs. Luce. Mrs. Helen Luce.

She had long blonde hair she tied in a braid, and she would talk to me after class every single day. She taught me how to stick up for myself. She taught me how to love myself, to believe in myself, to not let words hurt me. She was the first person who cared about me. She showed me how to let the Light in.

"Teachers like you save people like me. If it weren't for teachers like Helen, there's no telling where I'd be. I like you. There's something genuine about you, even if you have lied to everyone else you've ever met." She smiled. "There's something about you worth fighting for. There's reason to be hopeful. That's why I'm here. Remember that. I'll be back next week."

"One last thing. Do you believe in God?" Jasper asked. .

The CO checked his watch.

Angela showed him the ubiquitous gold cross dangling from the gold necklace that had been tucked inside her blouse, the same one he'd seen at Ray's more times than he could count. "I'm not a religious person, but I am a very spiritual person. I have faith in God. Do you?"

"I do now. Last night I prayed for a miracle, and He sent you."

She smiled. "If you worry, don't pray. If you pray, don't worry. Religion is for people who are afraid of going to hell. Spirituality is for people who are afraid of going back. You know the difference between belief and faith?"

"Tell me."

"Belief," she said, "is knowing that God is all-powerful and can carry a wheelbarrow on a tightrope stretched across the Grand Canyon."

Jasper stared at her.

"Faith is putting your ass in the wheelbarrow."

"That's it, Trueblood," the CO said. "Time's up."

"Thank you," Jasper mouthed toward the bulletproof partition, crying again. They pressed their hands palm-to-palm against the glass just as they had the last time at Ray's, in

Angela's former life as Ginger Snap. He heard her heels click as she walked down the hall, and as he returned to his cell, he recalled another verse of that Moody Blues song: *It's not the way that you say it when you do those things to me, it's more the way you really mean it when you tell me what will be.*

CHAPTER 16

THE YELLOW DRESS

Two hours after Miss Angela's angelic visitation, Jasper was in a mock courtroom with no ventilation and thirteen other inmates wearing KCJ-stenciled jumpsuits. His court-appointed public defender, an Asian man in gray pinstripes and shiny shoes, nodded a lot as he jotted things down on a yellow legal pad. Everything went pretty much as Angela had predicted. The man explained that this was just the plea, and the PD who would be representing the case in court would be meeting with Jasper a week or two prior to his court date. The man informed him that it was standard operating procedure to plead "not guilty," at least for now.

"Worst-case scenario, if I'm convicted, what kind of time would I be looking at?"

The man squinted at Jasper momentarily as if this might be a trick question. He set his yellow legal pad down and rubbed the stubble on his chin. "Under the circumstances, considering your clean record and favorable status in the community, you'd likely get about twelve months minus time served. If the girl hadn't died, you'd be out on personal recognizance by now."

Jasper tapped his foot and kept tapping it all throughout the ensuing arraignment. The judge was on a closed-circuit black-and-white television. She wore her reddish-brown hair with streaks of gray piled high on her head, french curls at her temples, and a sour scowl on her face. Jasper wondered if she were a mother and, if so, would she be less lenient because of it.

"Mr. Trueblood, you've been charged with possession of a Schedule II narcotic and child endangerment in the first degree. How do you plead on count one?"

"Not guilty, Your Honor."

"And on count two?"

"Not guilty, Your Honor."

"Very well, sir. The bail will be set at $12,000. You are required to pay ten percent of that amount to be released, which would amount to $1,200. Are you prepared to do that, sir?"

Jasper was transfixed by her face on the television. He did not have the heart to ask his father for that kind of coin; he was fresh out of resources. He made a mental note that the full bail amount was exactly what his biological mother had once willed him in her IRA. He wondered when the house would be seized.

"Mr. Trueblood?"

"Uh, no, ma'am. I mean, no, Your Honor."

The public defender argued for Jasper's release on his own recognizance. The judge declined. The public defender asked for a reduced bail, from $12,000 down to $5,000. The judge declined again.

"The trial is scheduled for Friday, May 29. Do you have any questions?" she asked.

"No, Your Honor."

"Very well, Mr. Trueblood. Good luck to you."

The next inmate was ushered up to face the TV, and a CO escorted Jasper back to his cell. As he walked, he did the math in his head. Nine weeks to find out what awaited the rest of his life, or at least the current facsimile thereof.

* * *

Delphi was lying supine on his bed, staring straight up at the bottom of Jasper's mattress.

"What up, homey? How'd it go?"

"First, I had a visitor, a black woman I used to know." Jasper cringed inwardly when he said it was a black woman, as if subconsciously this would impress Delphi. "It was a complete surprise. You would not even believe it if I told you how I knew her. Anyway, she explained everything, the whole process, and it all went down exactly as she described. It was like she choreographed the entire ordeal."

"You sound good. You got mo' pep in your step."

For the next several days, Jasper took Delphi's advice and tried to focus on staying busy. The prisoner known as Scarface liked to whisper "SOS" to Jasper in the mess hall, which Jasper found out meant "stab on sight." If Del was around, however, Jasper was safe.

The routine was wake up for chow at 6:00 a.m., clean the mess hall, swab the deck, straighten up the cell, and then hang out. Most of the men lifted weights, while some stayed in the dayroom playing dominoes, cards, checkers with chunks of milk cartons for pieces. Others were "court pulls," who met with attorneys and attended court proceedings. A lot of the inmates just went back to their cells and slept until lunch. Jasper had access to plenty of books in the library, though most of them were law books, not literature. He also had paper and a very small pencil the size of his pinky finger. He wrote poems that were full of angst and self-pity, laments about Rose, more grief therapy than poetry.

A Sonnet for Sweet Rose

I bet you'll never guess what happened to
     me today
I found my dear sweet Rose had left and
     gone far far away

She went without a warning, without even
     saying goodbye
She left us all perplexed and puzzled, con-
     founded as to why

Late at night, every night, I can hear her
     tiny call
She's wearing her favorite nightgown and
     holding little Snowball

But I realize this is nothing more than just
     a horrid dream
One where I forget how to cry and later
     how to scream

I hope with all my broken heart Miss Rose
     comes back someday
I'm on my knees and praying hard she'll
     return for her ballet

She was an innocent sweetheart, the pur-
     est form of life
Now here I am without her and it cuts
     deep like a knife

Forevermore I will always think about my
        dear sweet Rose
Who left this world much much too soon
        because of what I chose

Occasionally, there were extractions by the Special
Response Team, a gang of correctional officers dressed like
storm troopers, who would tear-gas a cell and eventually wheel
someone out in four-point restraints. Once, it was Scarface.

In the TV room, the pod boss and biggest gangbangers
decided what would be viewed, which usually meant sports.
Other programming favorites were *Cops* and *America's Most
Wanted*. Once Jasper tried to play basketball, but the brothers
took it a little too seriously. Still, even if he didn't play, Jasper
liked to assume the role of spectator because, although the
court was indoors, there was one open wall that afforded fresh
air and an expansive view of the sky. Razor wire was coiled on
top to remind would-be adventurers of the price for freedom.
Fresh air would be a commodity Jasper would never take for
granted again if he could just liberate himself from this god-
forsaken place.

* * *

It was exactly a week almost to the hour when Ginger Snap/
Angela made it back for another visit.

"How are you?" she said, her dimples and infectious smile
melting the glass between them.

"I'm surviving. You?"

"My kid has the flu. She's with the babysitter right now.
She's gonna be fine, but I had to keep her home from school."

"She's lucky to have you as a mom. Thanks for coming
back. I wasn't sure if you would."

She regarded him through the bulletproof glass like he was standing on a distant shore. "Yeah, about that, Professor. In the interest of full disclosure, I have a confession to make. You're not the only one who has struggled with addiction."

Jasper's eyebrows arched and his eyes widened. "You?"

"Look, I could have left Ray's a long time ago. I saved enough money for law school. After a while, I wasn't doing it for the money, I was doing it for the high. I was doing it for the same adrenaline rush you got from your drug, it's just that my drug was a behavior, not a chemical. I should have been home with Samantha.

"The thing is, for most addicts, addiction is just a symptom of something much deeper. I found out I had abandonment issues. I had issues with being molested in foster care. I used sex as a weapon. Addiction affects impulse control. It's like driving and wanting to stop but you have no brakes."

"What made you quit Ray's?"

She started twisting her security badge. "I tried to kill Ginger Snap a hundred times. I knew I didn't need the money, and I was unable to date anyone because I couldn't keep the personas separate and the stories straight. I haven't had intercourse with a man since my husband died. I was emotionally numb and didn't even realize it. Then one night, Sammie looked at me and said out of the blue, 'Mommy, how come your eyes are so dead?' That's when I decided to get out. I started seeing a counselor. I'm still seeing a counselor. I have to fix the shit from the past that's still broken. My therapist says I have to go backward to go forward."

Jasper thought he had long ago worked out all the issues from his own past, with being adopted as well as his father's volatile temper, but clearly there was still a lot of work left to do. He remembered he once wrote a poem called "Counterclockwise."

"You look especially nice today." Jasper smiled. "I like that skirt. Robin's-egg blue is a nice color on you."

She smiled. "C'mon, Trueblood, don't bullshit a bullshitter. How are you really?"

"Honestly." He swallowed hard. "Your visit last week is the only thing that has made my life bearable. Before that, I was mostly just . . . hanging on." He paused. "You know what worries me? I'm afraid that someday I'll forget her face, what she looked like. I'll stop feeling responsible for my part in this. You're right, Angela, it was an accident, but I should never have left the house."

"Professor, let me ask you a question. What would have prevented her from crawling out that window and falling into that fishpond even if you were at home? For example, let's say you were asleep in bed or in the kitchen making a tuna casserole?"

Jasper did not respond.

"It was an accident," she said.

"I know you're right, but I could have nailed the window shut. When I can't sleep, I think about that night. I think about how my life would be different if I had just stayed home. If I had made a better choice, she'd still be alive, her mother wouldn't be in jail, her father wouldn't want to kill me, and I'd still be teaching. My biggest decision of that day would have been relegated to what to have for lunch."

"First of all, the mother's already been let go. I'm not surprised no one informed you of that, but she was released and allowed to leave the state. She and the father took the girl's body with them."

Jasper's head dropped. "Thank God for that." A thought occurred to him—would Lani be able to survive Marcel's wrath? Would he go back to handcuffing and brutalizing her? Was she the next to die?

Angela continued, "If you had left dope on the table and she had ingested it, that'd be different. If you had left a weapon on the table and she shot herself, that would be different, too. There'd be blatant recklessness. A court would rule that as criminal negligence, and any reasonable juror would agree. But the girl snuck out a first-floor window. That is not the same. That's not the same at all."

Jasper's foot started tapping again.

"You can beat yourself up all day, but where's the bigger picture? It won't change anything. It's not going to bring her back. You have to release all hope for a better past. You can't make a better past, but you can make a better future. You owe it to yourself and the girl to live a productive life. The one thing you know for sure is that you can't change what's happened. Life is ten percent the shit that happens and—"

"Ninety percent what you decide to do about it."

She smiled. "You remembered."

"I remember everything you ever said to me. You're the smartest person I ever met. You're my sexual intellectual."

They both smiled.

"Five minutes," the CO announced.

For the last five minutes, they stared at one another with palms placed on either side of the bulletproof glass. But they did not speak.

* * *

On Mondays, Wednesdays, and Fridays there was a voluntary gathering called the Recovery Circle in which an addiction specialist, Ron, a tall man with a red beard and ponytail, shared his story of kicking heroin. In one anecdote about the night before he was scheduled to go to rehab, he was shooting black tar with someone in a park, "a last hurrah before D-Day." The other guy went first. After he pushed the plunger, he convulsed and his eyes rolled back in his head. He stopped breathing, and within three minutes, he was dead. "And you know what I did?"

Someone in the back said, "Did your shot?"

Ron nodded. "Damn straight. I took the needle out of his arm and stuck it into mine. The man had died. I knew that. But I didn't care. I was about to take a hypodermic needle and intravenously inject myself with the exact same poison that had just claimed the life of a fellow human being. Two thoughts occurred to me: it's so good, maybe I can get two shots out of it, and second, hurry up before cops come and think you killed this guy. So I did the entire shot, managed to leave before the police arrived, and the next day, my sister took me to rehab. Eighteen years ago and I still think about that guy." Ron shook his head. "Of course, for me, the first treatment center wasn't enough. The pain of changing hadn't surpassed the pain of staying the same. Less than a week into it, I walked out AMA— against medical advice. I had more research to do." He smiled and sipped his coffee. "When Johnny Law did catch up with me, it was the luckiest day of my life. I didn't realize it at the time, but they saved my ass. My entire existence looked like a windshield after a cross-country road trip. Nowadays, I don't think less of myself, I just think of myself less. Remember, in all this mess, there's a message. You don't have to live this way."

After Ron got the circle spinning, an invited guest or two, usually former inmates, contributed their experiences. Jasper was always amazed at the dichotomy, of how the stories were different yet the same. Finally, after the speakers, Ron saved "open time" at the end for inmates, some still in withdrawal and detox, to share their personal narratives. They were warned to avoid self-incrimination but encouraged to distinguish between self-investigation and self-justification. When they spoke, Jasper was able to see visions of himself, shadows and silhouettes, the ghost he had to exorcise once and for all.

"I was born needing a drink."

"The monkey's off my back, but the circus hasn't left town."

"At the end, it was like trying to push back the ocean with a blow-dryer."

"My six-year-old didn't trust me. She hid her piggy bank."

"I had a lot of resentments, so I injected poison in me to kill you."

"I hadn't slept in five days. I was paranoid and suicidal. I wanted to die, until I thought people were trying to kill me. Then I wanted to live so I could kill them."

"We're all here because we're not all there."

"I was terminally unique. I'm not much, but I'm all I think about. Don't you know who I think I am?"

"My life was shit surrounded by more shit."

"I felt like a left-handed person living in a right-handed world."

"I was a ghost. I could feel the wind whistling through me."

"I could fit all my worldly possessions into one large Hefty bag."

"I'm sick and tired of being sick and tired."

"The wheel was still spinning, but the hamster was dead."

"I kept looking at the mirror on the table instead of the mirror on the wall."

"I've lost everything in my life except my life."

"Delirium is a disease of the night."

"A lie doesn't care who tells it."

"I kept forgetting things, like not to steal a car."

"It's lonely in the gray-bar hotel, but it beats sleeping under a bridge."

"I couldn't imagine life with dope, and I couldn't imagine life without it. I was committing suicide a day at a time. Death in moderation."

"I knew I was allergic to alcohol because every time I drank, I broke out in handcuffs. I actually got used to being hog-tied in the back of a paddy wagon."

"My addiction was like having sex with an eight-hundred-pound gorilla. The sex was great, but it wasn't over until the gorilla said it was over."

"I was doing pretty well in college until my blood alcohol concentration became higher than my grade point average."

"I have to quit pissing on myself, and I have to quit pissing on my girlfriend. I've pissed on so many people."

"I'm a Picasso. The pieces are there but they're distorted as hell."

"As long as you changed everything exactly the way I told you to, I would accept you for exactly who you were."

"I woke up in four-point restraints not knowing if I had killed someone, tried to kill myself, or both."

"Every night was New Year's Eve, and my blood was eighty-six proof."

"I finally decided to do one of two things—either stop using or stop complaining about using. So, I stopped complaining."

"I had a hole in my heart where God used to be."

"My life was based on fear and single malt scotch."

"You're only as sick as your secrets."

"I didn't know how to feel about anything in life. I was emotionally retarded."

"I felt like a rainbow trout in a tank full of hammerheads."

"My ex told me to stop preying on people and start praying for them."

"I stood outside of the jail one night and pounded on the door to get in. I might be the first person in recorded history to break *into* jail."

"Isolation is a dark room where we go to develop our negatives."

"I was going to either jump in the Mississippi River and become a catfish or shoot enough dope to close my eyes once and for all."

"I finally hit my bottom at three a.m. in an alley with a prostitute lecturing me on how my life was out of control."

"They say insanity is doing the same thing and expecting a different result. Not for me. My insanity was knowing exactly what I was doing but doing it anyway. My life wasn't a roller coaster. It was that teacups ride at Disneyland. It just kept going around and around to infinity."

A Flathead Indian with a long black ponytail shared his story. "I'm a 0.35 drinker. Every time I end up in detox or the ER, I register at 0.35." He had the greatest last name Jasper had ever heard, *Terrence AliveWithSkies*.

Ron said that addiction came in three stages: (1) fun, (2) fun with consequences, and (3) consequences. He used big-picture words like *honesty, acceptance, willingness*, and *forgiveness*— simple words that in terms of diction now meant more than they ever had before.

"Recovery takes time," Ron said. "Time takes time. The jail cell you're housed in opens from the outside, but the jail cell in your heart opens from the inside." On the day that Jasper finally decided to relate his story about Lani and Rose, no one seemed to judge or condemn him. When he said that for the longest time, he just wanted to jump off the Aurora Bridge, people actually laughed—with him, not at him. They had all walked through the same fire. Afterward, as they were returning to their cells, Ron tapped Jasper on the shoulder. "The little girl? You might not believe this, but someday you'll realize she's already forgiven you."

* * *

"Del, you awake?"

"Yeah."

"You were right about keeping occupied and not dwelling on the outside, on what might have been. But do you ever get bored?"

"I get bored every day, homes. But I ain't trippin'. You got a mind. You got an imagination. You know what I'm sayin'? You can go anywhere you want in your head. Where you wanna go, cuz? If you could go anywhere right now, where you wanna go?"

"Uh, I don't know. Let's say . . . Australia. The land down under. I always wanted to go to Australia."

"Cool. Let's chill in Australia, mate. Come sit down here on the other side of the bed."

Jasper climbed down and they sat side by side.

"OK, bro, now fasten your seat belt, 'cause it's gonna be a bumpy ride." Del fastened his imaginary seat belt, and Jasper played along.

"You got your helmet strapped on tight?"

"Roger that."

"Five, four, three, two, one—*blast off!*" Del made a guttural sound that was as close to a rocket ship taking off from Cape Canaveral as anything Jasper had ever heard. He shifted the imaginary gearshift, stepped on the imaginary accelerator, and shook the bed. Jasper held on to the thin mattress for dear life. Del swiveled around, shuddered, and waggled until his entire body reverberated.

Jasper was laughing so hard his face was red.

"Tell me what you see, teach."

"I see a sign that says Welcome to Sydney. I see two kangaroos having sex while jumping up and down on a trampoline."

Now Del was laughing, too. "Good on ya, mate. What else?"

"I see Crocodile Dundee grillin' shrimp on the barbie. I see a wombat. I see Aborigines in the outback playing dice with a rattlesnake."

"There ain't no rattlers in Australia, teach."

"This one was smuggled in illegally by an exotic pet dealer."

Del laughed. "I gotcha. Keep goin'. What else you see?"

"I see a group of Boy Scouts singing 'Waltzing-fucking-Matilda' around a campfire and a billabong, and all the camp counselors are drunk as hell on Foster's Ale."

Delphi was cracking up. "Did I hear you right, mate? A dingo ate your baby?"

They were doubled over on the bed laughing and Jasper said, "Hey, Del, watch this." He took off a sock and made a sock puppet. "Hi, Del. My name's Bosworth. Wait, hey, no, no, Mr. Del, don't lock me in the trunk of the car, please, Mr. Del. Hey, Mr. Del, whatcha doin' with that gasoline? Mr. Del, put down that blowtorch!"

Del was laughing so hard he fell on the floor holding his ribs. He had to stand up and walk around the cell so he could breathe. He gave Jasper a high five. "You good, teach. You damn good."

That was the night Jasper knew that he could survive King County Jail no matter how long it took. His trajectory had straightened out enough so that at the very least he had something like hope.

* * *

It was Wednesday, April 29, and Jasper had been in King County Jail exactly thirty-eight days. Angela visited every week and kept reassuring him that he would not be in much longer, that she had hired her attorney to get angry for her. He read the King James Version of the Bible a lot—especially the psalms in the Old Testament, the parables in the New Testament, and he had a particular fondness for a paperback biography he found about St. Jude, the patron saint of lost causes. His favorite book of all, though, was a beat-up old 1978 edition of the *Merriam-Webster Dictionary* with the cover ripped off and several pages missing. He also did push-ups, sit-ups, and worked in the library with prisoners who were pretrial, wading through law books. One day he was assisting an African man with his resume. Under work experience, the man had written: *night stalker at a grocery store.*

Jasper explained that unless he meant *night stocker*, he should probably keep that information to himself. He explained the difference and they both laughed. He was reminded of his beloved Kiko and the difference between *stripping* and *shopping*. It made Jasper miss teaching terribly.

On April 29, after the evening meal, several of the inmates were creating a commotion by the TV.

"We interrupt this program for a special news bulletin."

In what seemed like milliseconds, every inmate crowded around until there was standing room only.

The Rodney King verdict was in. Four white police officers were acquitted by a jury that included no African Americans. Jasper could not believe what he was seeing. Within hours, LA was a third world war zone. Car windows were smashed by rocks and tire tools. Stores were looted. Fires were set. People were being pulled out of cars and beaten. The entire city was in complete chaos, and it was all being filmed like a Hollywood movie. Anarchy permeated every crack in every sidewalk, and the mood inside King County Jail mirrored what was on the tube. One side of the room would bellow "Fuck the police" while the other side responded with "No justice, no peace." The correctional officers congregated and conferred around the perimeter of the TV room. Ultimately, after a heated debate, they decided to allow the improvised rally to continue.

It was the first time Jasper truly felt fear. Scarface stared menacingly at him from across the room like T-Bone's crazy French-speaking dog, and with his right index finger made a slashing motion across his neck while mouthing the letters SOS, SOS, SOS.

"Go back to the crib," Del said. "I can't help you here."

Jasper hesitated.

"Now!"

At ten o'clock when the TV was turned off, the chanting continued as prisoners were forced to return to their cells.

Jasper and Del did not speak for two more days.

By the third day of the riots, May 1, May Day, the TV room was jam-packed from morning to night. In LA, revolution was the order of the day. Even a tearful Rodney King made an impassioned plea, dressed in a suit and looking forlorn, still not fully recovered but looking better than the last time he appeared on national television fourteen months earlier. After having been beaten so unmercifully in that now-infamous video, broadcast endlessly for days to every living room in America, King stood in front of microphones at a televised press conference pleading for peace. "I just wanna say, you know, can we all get along? Can we stop makin' it horrible for the older people and the kids?"

Bloods and Crips gathered and held a red bandana tied to a blue bandana. The same tone was prevalent between the gangs in the King County Jail.

On the fourth day, the same President Bush who took out Manuel Noriega in Panama a year earlier sent in four thousand military troops to join the one thousand federal law enforcement officers and National Guard to quell the madness. Mayor Tom Bradley and Chief of Police Daryl Gates made statements. That night, Jasper finally spoke to Del.

"May I ask you a question?"

"No." Then after a long pause. "OK, you can ask me one question. But just one, that's all."

"I know what they did to King was fucked up. He was on the ground long enough to cuff him. Everyone could see that on the video. They didn't have to keep beating him. But, Delphi, here's what I don't get. If you're a black man and you know that 'driving while black' can get you killed, why resist arrest? He led them on a car chase at over a hundred miles an hour. Once you're caught, why not just give it up and live to fight another day, especially if you know resisting arrest is gonna get you crippled or killed?"

"The brutha was fucked up on dust and was on parole. So he ran. That still don't mean you beat him like a rabid fuckin' dog."

"True, Del, but what gets lost in this riot is that black folks had the moral high ground. It was righteous indignation, and any reasonable person regardless of skin color could see that. Why set the whole city on fire? Why loot stores that belong to innocent people?"

"They didn't set the city on fire because of Rodney-fucking-King, bro. He's just the straw that broke the camel's back. They set the city on fire 'cause of all the other niggas who get fucked by the system for no reason at all, for all the other niggas who never did a damn thing but be black." Del stood up from his lower bunk. "Don't you get that, white boy? If you're white in this country, you've been raised with a silver spoon in your mouth since the day you was born. Are you too fucking stupid to get that?"

Jasper remembered Angela once said, in her previous life as Ginger Snap, that society reminded her every day that she was black.

"I oughta beat your fucking ass, you know that? Then maybe you'll know what it feels like to be nothing more than a tap-dancing show monkey in your sports stadiums. I'm sick and tired of playin' your super-Negro in here all the time and protecting your ass. Fuck you, muthafucka."

As Del approached with fire in his eyes, Jasper leapt off the top bunk. Delphi was between him and the cell door, so Jasper backed away toward the window. Delphi's fists were clenched. He advanced on Jasper in an attack position. "Maybe you oughta see what it's like to have people in your shit day and night."

"Del, man, come on. Please. We're friends. Del, please, don't do this."

Delphi suddenly sucker punched Jasper in the stomach.

Jasper doubled over and Delphi kneed him in the face.

There was blood dripping down Jasper's nose, lips, and chin.

"Muthafucka. I'm gonna end yo' bitch ass."

Jasper tried to look up just as Delphi was about to land another punch, but everything was a blur. He shouted desperately at breakneck speed, "Your sister's name is Marquita. She was in my English class. Last year. English 101. She wore a jean jacket and red Converse tennis shoes to school every day. She never missed class. *Marquita was in my class.*" Jasper could hear Delphi huffing and puffing but did not feel any more punches or kicks, so he continued.

"She wrote an essay called 'The Yellow Dress.' Her stepfather—*your stepfather*—raped her on Easter. She had a new yellow dress, not a hand-me-down from the thrift store. He also got drunk and burned her with cigarettes."

Del stopped, eyes wide and watery. He grabbed Jasper by the shirt and made a fist with his other hand. His eyes were wild like meteors. "'The Yellow Dress.'"

It was like Jasper had said the safe word.

"Marquita said the only person she could ever count on was her big brother. I'm assuming that's you. She said all she ever wanted to do was be a chef and cook for people. She said the main ingredient to any dish was love."

Del let go of Jasper. "She used to always say that." He caught his breath. "Shit, bro, you really did know her, huh? How come you never told me?" His chest was heaving.

Jasper cowered in his shadow as he approached again.

"Here, teach. I ain't gonna hit you no more. Let me help you up. I'm sorry, man. OK? I kinda lost my shit. I ain't slept since this Rodney-fucking-King thing started. But that was my bad, OK? Here, let me get you a towel for your face." Delphi wet a towel in the sink and handed it to Jasper. "I hope your nose ain't broke. If it is, just tell 'em you fell off the bed."

"I'm just tryin' to understand, Del. That's all. I can't imagine myself being you. I can only imagine myself trying to be you."

"I know, I know. You're on our side. You're teachin' Malcolm and Langston and Martin. But, bro, you gotta dig, too. This shit with the cops has been brewin' for a long time, and it finally hit the breaking point. Black folk been on edge since they kidnapped us four hundred fucking years ago and tossed our ass in a goddamn cargo ship. If you were a brutha, you'd be torchin' LA, too."

"Yeah," Jasper said, while dabbing at his nose with the bloodied towel. "I'm starting to get that." His eyes were watering badly; his face was throbbing like it had just been hit with a sledgehammer. Being a teacher for Del's sister had just saved Jasper's life. Helen Luce saved Angela's life. Jasper vowed to be a teacher again. Someday. Bosworth, too.

CHAPTER 17

LOVE IS AN ACTION WORD

"Trueblood!" the CO yelled out one morning just before chow.

Jasper climbed out of the top bunk.

"Bedroll and baggage!"

"Excuse me, sir?" Jasper said. "What did you just say?"

"Bedroll and baggage. C'mon, hustle up."

"For what?"

"It's your lucky day, Trueblood. You're being released. C'mon, roll it up."

Jasper's eyes widened. Was it an auditory hallucination, a trick, a prank, a joke? He waited for the punch line. It was four days after his thirty-third birthday, and if it was true, it was the best late birthday present in human history.

Del smiled that big reptile smile. "Check that shit out, yo. You're a free man, teach."

Jasper was in shock. He was afraid to ask what had happened, afraid that they would discover a clerical error, that they had the wrong cell in the wrong pod or had transposed a number and didn't want Inmate 54372 at all. *We were a digit off. Sorry for the inconvenience.* But he couldn't help himself. "Really?"

The CO nodded. "Really. You're not dreaming."

"Better, not bitter, right, boss?" Del said. He gave Jasper a massive bear hug and a high five.

* * *

What should have taken fifteen minutes of forms to sign turned into four hours of bureaucratic red tape, but Jasper was finally processed out and given a one-month bus pass to clinch the fait accompli. As it turned out, however, he wouldn't need the Metro. Waiting for him at the end of the cream-colored corridor was none other than his heroine, Miss Angela Brown.

There was no longer Plexiglas or bulletproof glass to separate them, so for the first time ever, he touched her—a brief but tender embrace. He was wearing the same clothes he had on the day he'd been booked, including the breath mints in his pocket and forty-two cents. The pants were a little loose. At least he had lost some weight. He dropped the stale cigarettes and lighter in a trash receptacle. When he saw the Swatch, he nearly started to cry. "I can't believe this is happening."

"Oh my God, are you all right?" she asked. "Your nose is swollen, and both your eyes are black. What the hell happened in there?"

"I'll tell you later."

They went down the elevator, and once in the foyer, Jasper took a final look around the place. They exited through the revolving door, and Jasper shielded his eyes from the detonation of sunlight. He stopped and stared at Angela. She smiled.

For a moment, they stood with fixed looks, and finally he stepped closer to her, then closer. He wanted to savor every instant, every moment. He leaned in and kissed her. To his surprise, she did not resist. He remembered what she once said about kissing, that it was the most intimate thing two people could do. It was slow and lingering, and she did not pull away. It was like the final kiss between a soldier and his sweetheart before he goes off to war or, better yet, the first kiss upon his return home. Like nothing else in the world mattered. Both oblivious that it was broad daylight, and they were making out on the steps of the county jail.

"Miss Angela, may I ask you a question?" He knew if he did not ask now—*right now*—he'd chicken out.

"Go ahead," she said a little breathlessly.

He looked deep into the pool of her eyes. "Will you be my girlfriend?"

She smiled. "Let's talk in the car."

They walked to the parking lot slowly, hand in hand, black and white fingers interlaced like piano keys, and when she unlocked the passenger door and let him in, he felt free and not in custody from cocaine or incarceration or sadness for the first time in a long time. She got in on the driver's side and they both sat silently for several minutes. She looked out the windshield and then in his eyes. "I'll answer your question, but I need to know something."

Jasper stared at her.

"Are you done?"

"With dope?"

"Yes, with dope. Because I have zero tolerance for street drugs. Zero. I'm a single mother about to start law school, and I don't have time for drama. I've got my own shit to manage. I have a daughter to protect."

"I'm done. I swear I'm done. How can I prove it to you? How can I convince you? Tell me what you want."

They laughed simultaneously.

"If you and I have a chance to be together, and maybe we do, then I have to be convinced beyond a reasonable doubt that you're really finished. Relapse and recidivism are real. They're powerful forces. I saw it with the girls at Ray's all the time. So, Jasper Trueblood, in my opinion, you need an army to fight this thing, and I took the liberty of finding you one."

"You found me an army?"

"Yes. The Salvation Army." Angela explained the drug rehab services offered by the Salvation Army and that they had a bed reserved in his name. There would be no cost, but in return for his lodging and meals, he would be required to wash dishes or work in the warehouse eight hours a day, five days a week, and attend recovery meetings daily.

"For how long?"

"Six months."

"Wow." Jasper paused. "Six months. That's a long time."

"Being healthy for the rest of your life is even longer. So . . . will you do it?"

Jasper nodded. "I'll do it for you."

"That's a place to start," she said, "but eventually you have to do it for you. As for us, talk to me in six months." She smiled. "I'll be waiting."

Jasper stared ahead at the dashboard.

"Hey." She smiled with her dimples and her diamond eyes and all her positive energy. She reached in her purse. "I almost forgot. I have a present for you." It was a small cardboard box with a white ribbon bow.

"What is it?"

"Open it," she said.

Inside was a tiny blue velvet pouch that tied with a gold string. He opened the pouch and extracted a diminutive piece of rock and a miniature scroll.

This official provenance serves to authen-
ticate that the stone contained herein is a
remnant of, and was extracted from, the
Berlin Wall in this year of our Lord, nine-
teen hundred and ninety.

"Wow." Jasper bit his lip, "I don't know what to say. Thank
. . . you . . . very . . . much." He laughed. "I assure you, the symbolism is not lost on me. The wall coming down?"

Angela smiled and slowly ran her soft fingertips down the
length of his left cheek. "I just saw this at the mall today, so I
got one for each of us. The symbolism is simply that the wall
between us, whether at Ray's or county jail, can be dismantled.
It just has to be slow and steady, one piece at a time."

"I read you loud and clear." He stared glassy eyed down
into his lap.

She leaned into him. "Look, if we're gonna do this, Professor,
we have to do it right. It's gonna take patience. You go through
the program, and then we'll talk about the next step. You have
to remember, I have a little girl at home, and she comes first.
After all this time she still misses her daddy, so you're gonna be
the *other* man in her life. My life, too."

He nodded. "I'm cool with that. When do I get to meet
her?"

"Samantha? In about twenty minutes. You ever eat soul
food before?"

Jasper said he had not.

"You curious to know how I finally got you out?"

"Yes."

They wheeled out of the parking spot and Jasper realized it
was real—it was all real.

"I got tired of their political brinkmanship, so I decided to
play hardball." Angela went on to explain how she managed to
make an appointment with the prosecuting attorney. He was

wearing lizard-skin cowboy boots, an Armani suit, and a pink silk tie. She informed him that his boss, the district attorney, was a regular customer at her former place of employment. She wondered if said boss, the district attorney, who was the prohibitive favorite in his run for reelection, would remember getting his rocks off by calling her a "dirty little whore," and further, would the district attorney care to see the surveillance tapes of him on multiple occasions walking around inside Ray's Pleasure Palace? She also told him that the district attorney once said that there were two kinds of women in the world, the kind who think with that thing between their ears and the kind who think with that thing between their legs. Would the DA like to be reminded of that little soliloquy? She also guaranteed the well-dressed prosecuting attorney in the expensive boots that if Jasper were not released within forty-eight hours, she would leak this information to her friend in the press, her former college roommate, who happened to be a TV producer at the local affiliate of a major network and who would be delighted to make this the lead story for the evening news. "I could call her for you right now if you'd like. How would your respectable DA's reelection campaign spin that one?

"Finally, I said, 'Counselor, this is the phone number to Ray's Pleasure Palace. Ask for Ray.' I wrote down Ray's number on this little scrap of paper, set it on Mr. Prosecutor's desk, and then walked out. That was yesterday. And guess what! Today, the very next day, less than twenty-four hours later, they magically decided to cut you loose. Imagine that," she said. They stopped at a red light. "Politics cuts both ways, Jasper, and the truth shall set you free. The good Lord giveth and the good Lord taketh away."

"Holy shit," Jasper said. "I'm glad I'm on your side."

She looked at her hair in the rearview mirror. "The prosecutor and I left on good terms. I mean, hey, who knows, maybe I'll work for him someday. No need to burn bridges, right?"

* * *

They drove to Angela's town house in the University District. Jasper met Samantha, admired her three Scholar-of-the-Month certificates, and saw a picture of her dad on the dining room wall. Jasper asked if there would be pigs' feet for dinner. Angela said there would not.

"Thank God," Jasper said.

She looked at him quizzically.

"It's a long story."

Angela poured herself a glass of 1966 Château Margaux, something she said she had been saving for a special occasion. Jasper and Samantha had glasses of Welch's grape juice. Then Angela served a feast of fried chicken, fried okra, macaroni and cheese, collard greens, and corn bread. For dessert, pecan pie with fresh whipped cream. Samantha talked about her softball team—she played second base—and her science project, and as she described her favorite teacher, Mrs. Popelka, Angela glanced at Jasper and flashed a conspiratorial smile.

After dinner, Samantha was in her room watching TV and fell asleep. Jasper took a long hot shower and was enjoying the steam when he heard a tap-tap-tap on the bathroom door. The door slowly clicked open. He wiped away the condensation from his side of the opaque shower door and saw her silhouette enter the bathroom. He was reminded for a moment of Ray's, but when her door slid open, suddenly, there was no partition between their faces, their race, their desire, no Plexiglas, no three inches of bulletproof glass. Their eyes locked on; she disrobed and unpinned her hair in back. Shook it out. Jasper remembered every square inch of the mocha skin she lived in, of how even in the ambient light of Booth 12 her dark skin glowed, her forehead, her cheekbones, the tip of her nose.

"This is your incentive to invest heavily in the next six months. I'm going to turn you on to a few of my girlish charms."

She stepped into the shower and joined him. She smiled. "I shaved my legs just in case."

They spent most of the next hour together getting exceedingly clean.

Later that night, he slept alone on the couch, dreamily thinking two things: (1) God bless Angela Brown, and (2) God bless her girlish charms. The next morning, he did not balk when she said it was time to go to his new home, and as they drove, he finally broke the silence. "I like saying your name, 'Angela Brown.' It has a nice cadence. Sometimes I say it in my head. It's poetry."

She smiled. "In high school, the boys called me 'Brown Sugar.'"

"Last night? That was the best shower of all time," Jasper said.

"There's a lot more where that came from." She winked (she had the best wink). "If you play your cards right."

"I have cards? Since when did I get cards?"

She smiled once again and held his hand as she drove.

* * *

One hundred and eighty days in drug rehab with nineteen other men was a lot to metabolize, but it was the right thing to do and infinitely better than KCJ. It was not altogether unlike jail—the clock and everything else being controlled by someone other than himself—but at least there were no cell doors constantly clicking, and the food was better.

When he wasn't working, sleeping, or in a recovery meeting with men chain-smoking and guzzling coffee—heavy on the cream and sugar—he spent most of his free time sitting in the chapel and writing in his notebook. Now and then, someone would be kicked out for sneaking booze or dope onto the premises. Early recovery was a precarious walk on the tightrope. Powerlessness and surrender to anything in life, much less addiction, were not concepts to which most people were open. Jasper learned that in terms of brain physiology, childhood trauma lived on the same street as chemical and behavioral addiction. He thought of dear old Dad.

The highlight of the week was when Angela and Samantha visited on Sunday afternoons. Sammie and Jasper would hang out in the game room and play foosball or bumper pool while Angela read. Sometimes all three of them would kneel in the chapel and pray. Angela met Mrs. McCready, who had generously stored Jasper's belongings in her basement, and he could pick them up anytime. Jasper's house was eventually sold at something called a "tax lien auction." Drug rehab was teaching Jasper not to regret the past but to learn from it, just as Angela had suggested. It stung a lot to lose the house that his biological mother had once given him, but he was grateful for this space, for his life, for air, for this moment in time.

One day, while lugging furniture out of the warehouse and restocking the showroom floor, Jasper saw a little Latina girl riding in a pink plastic princess car. "Please, Papa, please," she begged. "Can we please get it, Papa? Por favor?"

The father scolded her. "You know we don't have money for that. Put it back."

Jasper immediately remembered Chase's essay and the Latina girl he tried to save named Lucinda. Making his way up front, Jasper covertly slipped one of the cashiers a twenty-dollar bill. "Don't tell them it's from me," he said. He peeked from behind a rack of clothes as the cashier explained that, with the father's permission, a customer would like to purchase the car for his little girl. She started screaming and jumping up and down. The father had the trace of a reluctant smile, and Jasper realized he had never felt this good on cocaine.

That night after the evening meal, several men watched *The Lost Weekend* on the VCR. The movie starred Ray Milland as "Don the writer who can only write while drunk." Don goes on a binge, and even though the film was from the 1940s, the parallels to Jasper's life were unmistakable.

At a recovery meeting, one of the counselors said, "With real alcoholics like him, not problem drinkers but *real* alcoholics, the biggest problem isn't psychological as much as physical. The body craves alcohol. When it doesn't get it, the cells get agitated and everything turns to shit."

Another counselor said, "Learn to want what you have rather than complaining about what you don't. Be grateful for your blessings. When it comes to working your program, if you're coasting, you're probably headed downhill. Hell, last year over a million people worldwide died of dehydration, so stop bitching about whether the glass is half-full or half-empty. There's water in the fucking glass. That's all you need to know."

Yet another counselor elaborated on the difference between sobriety and recovery. "Sobriety," he said, "is just abstinence. If you take away the alcohol from the alcoholic, you still have the *ic*. All you have to change is everything. It's not a drinking problem, it's a thinking problem. You can't change the way you think to change the way you live—you have to change the way you live to change the way you think. Just remember these six words: trust God, clean house, help others."

All the rehab clichés were making sense. Jasper kept wondering how he got to where he was—an addict—by way of his old Analytical Psychology class, when what he really needed to tap into was his old Behavioral Psychology class. "Every time you get an urge to drink or use," the counselor said, "play the whole tape, not just the first scene. You have to think of the future in the present tense. It's not just one day at a time, it's one thought at a time. Replace that craving with something constructive like meditation or oil painting or playing the harmonica. Something constructive. Something you'll be proud of. Remember, the only person who uses the term *functioning alcoholic* is an alcoholic."

At an afternoon recovery meeting, there was a resounding, ear-splitting scream from the restroom down the hall. Everyone froze as a silver-haired man, Joseph, formerly a pill popper who had been in rehab the longest and was the acknowledged elder statesman, came rushing wide eyed into the meeting room. "Call 911," he said. "Hurry!"

"What is it?" the counselor said. "What's wrong?" He set his coffee on the floor and hurried back to the restroom. A new arrival by the name of Dennis, a homeless teenager and high school dropout, was lying on the floor with a hypodermic needle stuck in his left arm. His mouth was open, drooling. His body twitched with muscle spasms. His lips and face were a whitish blue, his breathing shallow and labored. "Holy fuck," the counselor said, checking for a pulse. "Jasper, call 911."

Jasper went for the phone in the other room, but even with the counselor performing CPR by pumping the victim's heart and the EMTs arriving in less than ten minutes, there was no saving Dennis. Everyone stood on the lawn as he was loaded by gurney into the ambulance.

Jasper felt a profound heaviness. *Rose.*

"Fuck," the counselor muttered under his breath to another counselor and then a little louder, "*Mother fuck.* If any of you thinks this shit is funny, tell me how funny it is now. Anybody who wants to leave, I'll gladly refund your misery." He kicked a shrub, which shed a halo of raindrops, and walked inside. Someone turned off the stereo and the lights. The recovery meeting was officially over. As Jasper walked back to the bedroom, one of his roommates said, "We don't shoot our wounded, but sometimes they shoot themselves."

* * *

The next few weeks were mercifully uneventful. In fact, Jasper had never felt better physically in his entire life. He was informed that once the body's toxins were expunged, there was a resiliency to the human anatomy that was nothing short of astounding. In early recovery, this was known as "the pink cloud."

Jasper was anxious to get back to teaching. Yes, he had once been charged with a felony, but on his job application, he could honestly answer no when asked if he had ever been convicted of one. He thought about teaching every day. Just to keep his hand in the game, not unlike tutoring at KCJ, he occasionally assisted men writing essays to complete their GED correspondence classes. On day thirty-three in rehab, he received his first phone call from someone other than Angela and Samantha. It was for "Junior McPherson, who also goes by the name Jasper."

"Hello?"

"Junior? I mean, Jasper? This is Father Ross from St. Martin's in Belleville."

"Father Ross, how are you? What a surprise!"

"Junior, I'm afraid I have some bad news. Your father died three days ago."

"Dad died?" Jasper paused. There was an extended silence. He said quietly, "What happened?"

"I'm afraid he had a heart aneurysm. He had been deteriorating for a long time, Junior. I tried to find you, but it was difficult. Bob told me you had some legal issues, but it was hard to track you down."

Jasper was listening intermittently, drifting in and out, missing every other phrase. "I'm sorry, Father. I got caught up in drug addiction. I shouldn't have called him, but I needed to post bail. He sounded so lost on the phone that I didn't call him back. I should have. I really should have. I was hoping to visit him, to surprise him once I got out of drug rehab." Jasper stared at the wall.

"Junior, I know you and Bob had a tough time of it after your mother died, but I hope you know how much he loved you. In his own way, he really did. Bob revealed something to me as he was going under anesthesia that explained a lot of his temperament. He never told you this, I'm sure, but I think you should know."

Jasper sat down on the floor. He could feel the numbness setting in again, like he was going under anesthesia himself.

"Many years ago, when Bob was in the navy, something terrible happened."

"You mean in the war?" His father had always maintained he had not seen any significant action.

"No, not in the war. On shore leave. Several sailors sexually assaulted your father. Your mother knew, but she was the only one. He never told anyone else. When he was recovering from his surgery, I asked him if what he had said when he was going under was true. He said it was. He asked me if I thought he had committed a sin. I told him of course not, but those sailors did. He was consumed with shame. He carried that around his entire adult life. It explains a lot of his rage. Religion is one thing, but he needed psychotherapy. That kind of assault can lead to progressive trauma. For someone like your father, it can't just be prayed away. He needed help."

Suddenly, all the years of his father's rage and fury made sense.

"Junior, are you still there?"

"Yes, Father."

"The funeral is Saturday morning, day after tomorrow. Your father left you a few personal items and about $750. Would you like to fly back for the funeral? I mean, are you allowed to leave rehab for something like this?"

"I'm sure I can work it out. The counselors here condone that kind of thing. I'll be there."

"The Mass is at St. Martin's at nine. Afterward, we will head out to Mount Carmel. He finally gets to be buried next to your mother, Junior. He's waited for that for a long time."

Jasper's voice cracked. "OK, thanks, Father Ross." It felt cleansing when Jasper went back to his room and finally allowed himself to cry. What Angela had once said in Ray's about neuroplasticity was coming true. Jasper Trueblood was learning how to feel emotions again.

* * *

He told Angela the whole story of his father's temper and propensity toward violence, of how he once whipped Jasper with a belt for taking a bath instead of a shower like a real man, whipped him so hard there were thick red welts on the backs of his legs, and he couldn't go to school for two days. She hugged him hard. Jasper also explained to Angela that he had never fully understood or appreciated all the sacrifices Robert McPherson had made until now: his father never went to bars or restaurants, on vacations, to dinners or ball games or movies . . . His father never did much of anything except provide for his family and try to please Doris McPherson.

"May I ask you a question?" Jasper said.

"Of course," Angela replied tearfully.

"Did you ever forgive your mother for leaving you in that phone booth back in Nashville?"

Angela laughed a little. "Yeah." She paused then. "It took some time, but I forgave her." She wiped her eyes. "I wasn't going to, and then I read this goddamn quote supposedly by Mark Twain, 'Forgiveness is the fragrance that the violet sheds on the heel that has crushed it.' When I read that, I realized what I had to do. My birth mother still had this dark power over me, this . . . negative energy. I had to let all that shit go. Hatred is exhausting. I made peace with it a long time ago. But unlike you with your biological mother, I was not inclined to find her. What's done is done, you know?

"A few years ago, not long after my husband died, I wrote her a three-page letter, single-spaced, then Sammie and I drove halfway up Mount Rainier. We found a little waterfall, got out of the car, and I read the letter. When I finished reading, I lit it on fire with my Bic lighter and sent the letter up to the heavens."

Jasper nodded. He loved looking at her.

"And guess what. As I was driving home, we pulled off the road to fill the gas tank and get some lunch. We're walking into this little roadside diner and what did I see on the horizon? The most spectacular rainbow ever, this massive semicircle across the sky. And you know most of the time with rainbows you can't see the whole thing, you can only see part of them? Well, this time, you could see it in its entirety all the way from end to end. That's when I knew she got the letter, and that's when I knew everything was going to be OK. I felt like Noah must've felt after the flood."

Jasper thought immediately of Rose, of the transom-prism poster with the rainbow projected on her. Her own personal rainbow. Just like Angela's. Just like Noah's after the flood. Maybe Ron back at KCJ was right. Maybe the little girl had already forgiven him.

"Will you go to the funeral with me? My father left me enough money to pay for our plane and hotel. We fly there tomorrow, go to the funeral Saturday morning, and fly back home Saturday night. Maybe you can get a sitter for Samantha? Maybe you can—"

"Yes, yes," she said and hugged him hard. "Of course, I'll go."

Neither relinquished the embrace for the longest time, and it was at that very moment Jasper became aware of something quite remarkable, that he had never felt so close to another human being. Even more remarkable was the fact he wasn't terrified by it.

Angela whispered one last quote in his ear. Oscar Wilde. One of her favorites. "'The only difference between the saint and the sinner is that every saint has a past, and every sinner has a future.' That's you and me, Professor. Saints with a past. That's where we live."

* * *

On Friday morning, the babysitter came over with a suitcase to stay with Sammie overnight. Jasper and Angela flew back for the funeral, rented a car in St. Louis, and as they drove over the suspension bridge atop the choppy brown waves of the old Mississippi River, Jasper said hello to Troy Archer below.

It was dark and drizzling by the time they arrived in Jasper's hometown, Belleville, Illinois, home of tennis star Jimmy Connors. Jasper drove Angela past the old house where he had grown up, his old grade school and high school, the bars he drank in, the hospital his mother died in. In the hotel room, Angela held him close until they drifted off to sleep. The next day it was pouring so hard that they got drenched just running from the rental car to the church vestibule.

Jasper kept thinking about shame. That was what he and Bob had in common, more than anything else. It would take time to work on that. He looked at his Swatch.

After the funeral Mass, they drove to the cemetery in the rental car behind the hearse. When they arrived, relatives and other mourners were gathering around the large canvas tent draped over the burial site. Jasper noticed they were all staring at Angela.

She whispered in his ear. "Have they ever seen a black person before?"

He scanned their faces. "No. You're the first." He smiled and reached out to hold her hand. Her eyes were coppery-yellow and hypnotic. He had never seen eyes like Miss Angela's.

Bob would be buried in a plot adjacent to Jasper's mother. Jasper hadn't seen Doris's headstone or read the inscription since the last time he saw his father alive, which ironically was right here in Mount Carmel, at this gravesite, over a decade ago.

> In memory of our dearly departed
> DORIS LYNN McPHERSON
> Born: October 20, 1930
> Died: December 2, 1978
> from her loving family

There were wilted white roses on her grave. Sometimes Jasper wondered if his father had ever felt guilty for loving her more in death than he had in life or, perhaps more important, if he had ever forgiven himself. Jasper knew firsthand it was no small task to forgive the sins of the self. But this was no time to be judgmental; his father was finally at peace. A man started playing the harmonica, and the woman next to him began singing.

"Amazing Grace, how sweet the sound . . ."

Jasper remembered Del's story about the slave ship captain. His eyes watered. He touched the gold cross around his neck, a recovery gift from Angela, identical to her own. He kissed the cross. She saw this and leaned into him.

"You're gonna be OK," she whispered. "I love you."

The words seemed to rebound off the headstones and resound through the trees, and Jasper had the distinct feeling that somehow, it was his father from the great beyond who had orchestrated the search party in the form of Father Ross.

Jasper needed to be at this funeral. For some unknown reason, Jasper felt unexpectedly at peace.

Under the tent, with the rain pelting down on the canvas above and the smell of fresh dirt in the air, Father Ross quoted some of Bob's favorite scriptures, including: *Love your enemies* and *Pray for those who persecute you.*

A few years later, as an homage to his father, Jasper would have his right forearm tattooed with the famous lines from Dylan Thomas, lines the poet had written to his own father: *Do not go gentle into that good night* and *Rage, rage against the dying of the light.*

With Angela's arm hooked into the crook of his elbow, Jasper watched as the cemetery workers lowered the casket into the grave until it touched down. Father Ross said some final words. Jasper shook hands with the good padre, then thanked friends, relatives, and well-wishers from the parish for coming—no, he could not stay, he was flying back to Seattle that day—and some of them still had their eyes affixed on Angela. Jasper looked at her and she squeezed his arm.

As they cruised in the rental car back to the airport, Jasper turned off the radio and they drove in silence for several miles until he said, "Mr. James at the Salvation Army would like me to mentor some of the new guys. He wants me to stay on another six months. That would be a whole year."

"Are you going to?" Angela asked.

"I think I should. I want to work on my recovery at least as hard as I worked on my addiction, but I also want us to be a couple, you know?" They were stopped at a train crossing. He looked at her. "I love you."

"I love you, too, and if you play your cards right, we will be together."

"Again with the cards? I love these cards."

She smiled. "The best way for us to be a couple is for you to make recovery your number one priority. You know what I mean?"

The train passed and the crossing arm lifted to allow traffic. "Will you and Sammie still visit me?"

"Ha, just try to stop us." She nestled up against him and drifted off to sleep.

The rain finally let up and plum-colored clouds wafted by. As the rental car crossed the old Mississippi, Jasper remembered him and Bud Black sailing Troy Archer's ashes on that raft downriver toward New Orleans.

Several hours later, on the plane, Jasper was still peering into the black sky, into the tuxedo of night, holding the velvet pouch with the chunk of the Berlin Wall for good luck, Angela with eyes closed, breathing rhythmically beside him. Just before takeoff, the flight attendant had made an announcement to all the passengers in Jasper's row, though she seemed to be speaking directly to him.

"Good evening, folks. You are seated near an emergency exit. This is a new feature of our aircraft, and we ask that you carefully read the special instruction card located in the seat pocket directly in front of you. If you do not wish to perform the instructions in the event of an emergency, I'd be happy to reseat you."

Jasper smiled.

"Will you be OK, sir?"

"Yeah. I'll be fine." He smiled.

After takeoff, he began to peer out the window at the constellations and star clusters and remembered how, a few months after Lani and Rose had arrived on the scene from Guam, Jasper had returned home one night after teaching an evening ESL class. Usually, Rose ran up to him with a big hug and the requisite "You'll never guess what happened to me today," but this particular night, her gaze was fixed out the picture window in the living room. He called her name, but still, she did not turn her little head with the silky black hair like her mother's, and Jasper became immediately worried about a potential prowler. He walked over, pulled back the curtains, and searched but saw nothing unusual. "What are you looking at, little girl?" he asked.

Without taking her eyes from the sky, she said, "I'm counting the stars."

Jasper almost laughed but caught himself. "And how many stars are there, Rose?"

She turned toward him and said in the smallest, most serious voice he had ever heard, "Over a million."

From the window seat of an emergency exit row of Flight 187, nonstop St. Louis to Seattle, Jasper Trueblood gazed at the firmament and glared at the moon until his eyes watered, just like when he was a kid. And it occurred to him that when it came to counting stars, Rose's response—*over a million*—might just be the best answer in human history.

ABOUT THE AUTHOR

 Michael G. Hickey received a BA in creative writing from the University of Arizona, 1987, and an MFA from the University of Washington, 1992. In 2009, he was inaugurated as Seattle's eighth *Poet Populist*. His first novel in The Trueblood Trilogy series was *Counterclockwise*, the second is *Tell Me What You Want*, and the third installment is tentatively due for publication in 2022. Hickey has also published three books of poetry and prose, *A Dress Walked by with a Woman Inside*, *In Defense of Eve*, and his newest title, *How to Talk to Girls (& Other Urban Myths)*. In his spare time, he volunteers as a creative writing instructor for children at bereavement camps, juvenile offenders at youth detention, and adult inmates in federal prison.

Made in the USA
Columbia, SC
19 May 2021